ONE TIME, BADLY

Allyson Souza

Karen,
I hope you found good company in Cecelia & Max! Thank you for the lovely discussion and insightful questions. It was so great meeting you!
-Allyson Souza

Copyright © 2020 Allyson Souza

All rights reserved

The characters and events portrayed in this book are fictitious. Any similarity to real persons, living or dead, is coincidental and not intended by the author.

No part of this book may be reproduced, or stored in a retrieval system, or transmitted in any form or by any means, electronic, mechanical, photocopying, recording, or otherwise, without express written permission of the publisher.

ISBN-13: 9798629694861
ISBN-10: 1477123456

Cover design by: Christina Rafanello
Library of Congress Control Number: 2018675309
Printed in the United States of America

For my parents

CHAPTER 1

**2018
September**

She'd been thinking the same thing all day. From the moment she'd untangled her legs from her bed sheets and rolled towards the edge of the mattress, with that determined wave of anxiety snaking its way through her stomach, Cecelia had known. That familiar voice, whispering its way through three years of hard-fought progress, was already telling her to just stay home. But what could she do?

She shook it from her mind as she dressed for work, as she packed an extra bag with her change of clothes for the party that night, as she rode the bus, then ordered a coffee from the food cart on the corner. *Black today. Yes, I'm sure.*

She was hoping for a shock to the system, hoping for anything to knock the thought from her mind. But that voice telling her that she definitely shouldn't be doing this, that *absolutely* no good could come from this, just wouldn't go away.

It nagged her through two meetings and one very trying conference call, it tried to persuade her not go as she changed into the vintage silk slip dress she'd picked up the week before and slipped on her one and only pair of expensive heels, Manolo Blahnik's a la Carrie Bradshaw. When she went for her favorite shade of lipstick it flat out panicked. That shade, with its sultry notes of burgundy bordering on red, could only mean one thing.

But it was now, as she exited her office building, that the voice really and truly lost it's shit. It was begging, it was on it's knees with hands clasped tightly in front of itself as it willed her towards the subway that would take her back to Port Authority, to a bus that would take her safely home to New Jersey. Nevertheless, Cecelia lifted her head and squared her shoulders. It was with a determined step that she turned in the opposite direction and began her walk uptown.

It was a cool night in New York City. Just at the edge of September, this weather always reminded her of pencil shavings and worn textbooks. The hint of crispness to come brought her right back to days spent wandering quads and soaking in the last few weeks before fall semester took a turn for the cold and she was left rushing from her dorm to the warm reprieve of her classroom.

Not that she minded. There was something comforting about the cold air, something startling and refreshing and altogether romantic. The sound of dead leaves scratching along the ground and crunching under busy feet was rhythmic, it was conversational. And, in her opinion, it just seemed to smell better than any other season.

She was thankful that she wasn't battling the suffocating density of a humid summer night as she walked toward this moment, with all of its threatening possibilities. Yes, she'd always loved this time of year. She was grateful that she still managed to feel that way, despite everything that had happened. But then, he'd loved it, too. Hadn't he?

2011
September

Cecelia Scott had been wandering around this party for over an hour now, spotting her brand new friends, their faces still unfamiliar for a split second, here and there. She was doing her best to strategically use that split second to plaster a nice, big I'm-having-so-much-fun-aren't-you? smile on her face before anyone caught her staring longingly at the door. She'd quickly grown sick of the warm beer and loud voices, but didn't want to leave and risk missing out on *the* moment that everyone would talk about for the rest of the weekend.

She'd put on the tight dress, spent an unnecessary amount of time following a YouTube tutorial entitled "Perfect Party Makeup in 10 Minutes!" (45 minutes for the artistically inept), and even managed to work her long, chestnut locks into some "sexy" waves. It had all come together; she was College Party Girl – successfully navigating the treacherously narrow, inevitably beer-soaked stairs leading to any frat house basement, and in heels no less! And now she was testing how many hours she could stand in said heels, not quite buzzed and too bored to keep feigning interest in the aggressively long beer pong game happening before her.

She spotted a deck where a few people were standing around smoking in small groups and quickly navigated through the packed kitchen to reach the swinging screen door that led outside. The fresh air felt like heaven against her sweat-dampened skin, and she seriously considered taking up smoking just to avoid the actual party portion of going to parties.

Four seconds into that thought pattern she dropped it, already hearing her mom's disapproval – not that the familiar voice in the back of her head had kept her from attending this party in the first place. One of the most important lessons she'd learned at Rutgers University was when to let the chatter in the back of her head affect her decisions and when to tune it out all together.

It was more difficult to ignore when she'd been a freshman the year before. When she left her small town for RU, she promised herself that she would step out of her shell. She was faking it until she made it. Pretending to like parties and shots of cheap liquor and frat basements because that's where the fun was.

The way Cecelia saw it, memories were made in all of the

places that made her a little uncomfortable. She had four years to live this way, and then she could go back to her books and Gilmore Girls with the knowledge that she'd tried it.

She was learning what she'd been missing, so she wouldn't have to wonder if she was missing out anymore. She wasn't always having the most fun, but at least she was inviting the chance for something new to come along.

She walked to a clear space and leaned against the railing, looking out over the other houses on the block. She could see similar scenes to the one she was currently a part of in various other yards on the block and the next one over. She focused on the closest one, trying to see if there was another girl bored and alone on a deck nearby, or if she was the only college sophomore who would rather be sleeping at 12:30 am than breathing in secondhand smoke and sipping on cheap beer that could only be described as piss warm.

At least it was a nice night. Just on the cusp of October, the heat had fully left the air, making way for a barely-there crispness that promised red leaves and an excuse to pull on her warmer sweaters. Her dorm room would still find a way to be as hot as Hades tonight, she'd bet money on that. But she was *this close* to relief from the torture that is the first month of fall semester in a building with no AC.

Cecelia was trying to appreciate the novelty of sophomore year of college while it still existed. She had the tendency to wish away these first few weeks in her haste to get to the middle of fall semester. There was nothing she loved more than the point when she was familiar enough with her professors and classmates that even this huge university felt as warm and comfortable as her high school classes had. And then the weather would get nasty; this was New Jersey, after all.

Classes during spring semester always felt a bit like a trap, all of that beautiful weather and so much to do with it. Open quads to lie out on, drinks to be had in backyards and on rooftops, iced coffees to gossip over. But not fall semester. Once November hit, classrooms became little havens. No one was lingering outside the building doors just trying to get a few more minutes of sun and fresh air. The bustle to get indoors was amazing, the heated air like a gift to red cheeks and stiff fingers.

Her classes seemed interesting, too. Her schedule was light on math and science, thank the Lord, and full of English courses, which she'd pay for later, but she wasn't going to think about that right now. She'd gotten through freshman year with a 3.8 gpa and without the freshman 15. As far as she was concerned, she deserved a reward and one wholly enjoyable semester was it.

She looked down at her half empty cup and considered her options. She could refill it and give this night another chance, or she could call it right here, right now. She didn't have eyes on any of the girls she came with, all of whom were new friends from her dorm building with the exception of her roommate from last year, Lou. She figured at least a few of them would be willing to go so she didn't have to walk back to the dorm by herself. It was at least a 10-minute walk, which was nine minutes longer than her parents would approve of on the walks-through-campus-at-night front. The voice was low, but always there.

She hadn't even noticed that he was there until he spoke.

"Well, it doesn't look like you're having any fun right now. And, damn, I spent almost sixty bucks on all these very inconspicuous red solo cups. Please don't tell me I wasted that small fortune on a lame party," he was failing to hold the serious look on his face, quickly giving way to one of the most endearing smiles she'd ever seen. It was funny how quickly a cute boy could make a girl forget her boredom, make her forget her aching feet.

"I'm the wrong girl to judge the caliber of a party off of. I think this one happens to be a little out of my league, so compliments to you, purchaser of the cups."

This was the truth. She loved going out when the group was small, and the music wasn't so loud. She always got a little overwhelmed by the mass chaos of the fraternity houses; it was something she'd figured she'd outgrow after some time, but she now accepted as her own preference.

"Nah this party is lame, you're out of its league," he was leaning against the railing beside her, looking out over the yard as well, giving her the perfect view of a strong jaw line and even stronger bicep. He was clearly taking advantage of the bevy of free gyms that Rutgers offered.

"I'm Nathan, by the way." He reached across his body, sticking out his hand in an oddly formal gesture for a beer-coated deck in the heart of New Brunswick, New Jersey.

"Oh, I'm Cecelia, it's –" whether she was going to tell him it was nice to meet him or try to defend his party again she never could remember. At that very moment, when she could have very well been meeting a man worth knowing, her back was drenched in what must have been the only cold drink at the entire party.

She spun on her heel, fully awake now, and found herself eye level with a short, scruffy guy, probably a year or two older than herself. His cup was still tilted in her direction, a mouthful of amber liquid lapping up the side and back down again from the commotion.

"Sorry, man! Didn't mean to soak you like that! My bad," his droopy eyes slid even further closed during his apology, making it difficult to tell if he even knew which one of them he'd spilled his drink on.

"Actually, that was my bad. I knocked this little punk in the shoulder. Thought he could handle it. Also my bad." He was tall. That was the first thing she noticed about him. She had to bend her head back just to meet his eyes. Which were the second thing she noticed about him.

He had the bluest eyes she'd ever seen on another person. Pale and bright at the same time, they looked almost translucent in the moonlight. He stood behind Droopy Eyes, clutching his own red cup absentmindedly in one hand and balancing a lit cigarette between the middle and index finger of the other.

"Don't worry about it, no big deal," she spoke the words,

feeling more awkward by the second as the liquid slowly warmed against the heat of her skin.

"You can't walk around like that for the rest of the night. We don't want word getting out that girls that come to our parties get treated badly. I think between me and Nate we can find you something to wear."

CHAPTER 2

2011
September

She was honestly never coming to a party again. She was bad at parties, College Party Girl she was not. And now she was following this complete stranger to what she could only guess was his bedroom, leaving all of the noise and people behind. She had two choices; it was either tune out the voice in the back of her head, or bolt like hell towards the front door and scurry back to her dorm room reeking of beer for all of the Resident Assistants to see.

He seemed nice enough. He was friendly in his offer of fresh clothes, no leering or creepy comments about her body in the already-too-tight dress, which was now slightly see through for having been made wet. And he didn't seem that drunk, definitely not drunk enough to be aggressive. But, that only applied if he wasn't aggressive to begin with. Some men didn't need alcohol for that.

As if he could read her mind, he interrupted her increasingly frantic train of thought with an apologetic smile, "I'm really sorry about your dress, I hope it's not ruined or anything," he made a quick turn and led her up another flight of stairs. "I should've just grabbed something and ran it down to you instead of leading you through this maze."

"It's all right, this house is huge though, I didn't realize there were so many floors," the small talk was making her feel a little better.

"Yeah, when there are so many people here it feels a lot smaller than it actually is. It's not a bad deal, as long as you don't mind the smell of weed and dirty socks all day, every day. Kinda makes me wish I'd joined a frat."

"Oh, I thought you lived here?"

"Nah, my buddy's in this frat, I wasn't really into the whole paid brotherhood thing, but the parties are usually pretty fun," when they finally reached the end of the hallway, he opened the door to a surprisingly neat room, and quickly began rummaging through the bottom dresser drawer. "He's gotta have something to at least get you home and past the RA's without broadcasting where you were."

"Like I said, it's really not necessary. I can just have one of the girls that stayed in run a hoodie out to me or something," she was just now realizing that accepting his help meant that she'd be spending the rest of the night walking around in men's sweats and these ridiculous heels. Disaster.

"Oh yeah, and did a lot of your friends ignore their raging FOMO and chill in the dorms tonight?" she could hear the mix of triumph and playfulness in his voice.

He definitely wasn't wrong about that. She couldn't think of one person that she was close enough with to ask a favor of that wasn't in this very frat house right now.

"Honestly, not surprised at how well you have us college girls pinned," she quirked an eyebrow at him, waiting to see what he said to that.

She was confident that her nudging wasn't far from the truth. He looked like he'd just walked off a movie set in 1955, old-school handsome. He definitely wasn't struggling when it came to the female population of Rutgers University, she'd bet money on that.

He was the boy you noticed on the first day of class and did an internal cheer because, even on the most boring of boring days, there was a distraction sitting just a few seats away.

He had the slight physical imperfections that only added to his attractiveness, rather than taking away from it. She'd already noticed a few scars on his face, a slight tip to his slightly too-big nose.

"Hey now, don't try to call me out in my own best friend's frat house!" He was trying really hard to balance both fake-indignation and fake-anger on his face. "Did you consider that the only reason I'm not in bed watching Sports Center at this very moment is because men, too, suffer from FOMO? I'll have you know, my throat was hurting all day, but I powered through. Because, I'm a man. And I was afraid that everyone would have fun without me."

And there was her proof. 'Grace under pressure' is what she and Lou would call it, and you'd be surprised at the amount of men that would shoot a look her way at that comment, as if to say, "Just look at me. Yeah, I know about girls." Then there were the ones that completely folded, so unfamiliar with flirting that they could come up with exactly nothing which to say in response. She had live action here, though.

"You had a sore throat *all day*, but you still came to this frat party? You're an animal, so manly," she played back. She might not have a ton of experience with guys, but she was smart, and that could get a girl further than most other things.

"Yeah, well it's a good thing I came, too. Otherwise you'd be sitting your pretty little behind in AA meetings for the next 3 weeks," she didn't mention that she'd already endured that punishment last semester when she got caught taking shots in her dorm room before Rutgers' Springfest. A smooth criminal, she was not. The consequences were worse for the second offense, hence her current situation.

"Sending the FOMO gods all of my love and appreciation for ensuring your presence at this event. What's your name? I want to make sure I include it in my mental thank you note," she clasped her hands together in mock prayer.

"Very thorough of you. I'm Max," he finally stood up from the drawer, pushing down the mess he'd made of it and slamming it shut with a swift shot from his Nike-clad foot.

"Hello Max, I'm Cecelia, such a pleasure to meet you," she offered him her hand and he took it, swallowing it completely in his own. They both adopted serious faces, and gave a firm pump at the elbows as if they'd just closed on a million dollar business deal.

"You know what, Cecelia?" he dropped the stern look, smiling all the way up to his eyes. She could tell from the excited quirk of his lips that he was about to say something that he knew was cute, something designed to melt her just a little bit. "I think from now on I'll call it FOMO on Cecelia."

"FOMO on Cecelia? That doesn't sound good at all."

"Fear of Missing Out on Cecelia. It'll get me to every party this year."

With that, he flashed her a smile, handed her some wadded up clothes, and walked out of the room leaving her feeling like butter on warm bread.

2018
September

She knew she should've just hailed a taxi. Her feet were already starting to ache and she'd only walked two blocks. She still had twenty-one more to go and things weren't looking good for her squished toes. But there was something that pushed her forward.

Maybe it was the bustle of the strangers around her or the peaceful night air, but something kept her from taking the easier route to the restaurant. Or maybe it was a way for her to have control over something about this night. Because once she walked into that party, all bets were off.

All day, she'd questioned her decision to put herself in this position, to risk opening old wounds that were so newly healed. It had taken her years, *years*, to feel like herself again. Or to become a person who was okay with her past, who could let go of the turn it had all taken and feel the peace that she'd taken for granted for the better part of her twenty-six years.

But she knew it would be awful for her to skip this particular event, even if Lou had not very convincingly told her it wasn't a big deal. There aren't a lot of things a person who'd heard you cry yourself to sleep every night for an unmentionable amount of time wouldn't do to help you keep your balance. Even if it meant that her maid of honor would miss the very first celebration of her brand new engagement.

Albeit, a casual celebration. The family party, with all of its formalities and heartfelt speeches would come later. Tonight would just be a few friends going out for drinks, raising a glass to two people who just might be the easiest couple to root for in the whole lot of them. Joe and Louisiana hadn't had a clear road to this night, and Cecelia wasn't going to put a damper on it. She knew, no matter what she may have said, that Lou would be disappointed if Cecelia wasn't there. She'd understand, as best friends tend to do, but she'd be sad and it just wasn't worth it.

This was a band-aid that would need to be ripped off eventually. From the sound of it, this was just the first of many events that this particular group of people would share. Lou wasn't the type to do anything halfway and her wedding would be no exception. She'd host dinner parties and she'd already said she felt like maybe they should do two rehearsals, because who could trust Joe's friends to pay attention the first time.

And so Cecelia never faltered. She told Lou that she was being ridiculous for even suggesting that she miss such a big moment in her life. What kind of friend did she think she was? But, even as the words left her mouth, as Louisiana squealed and shot her ring that longing look, Cecelia felt the panic begin to rise.

Panic had become familiar to her in the past few years and she could almost always fight it away. She could take a moment in her own mind to remember the things that were steady, all around her. Of her parents' voices and her childhood bed, of her sister's laughter and the warmth of the Labrador, Ensa, they'd gotten just as Cecelia had graduated from middle school.

She'd think of her legs moving fast, headphones blaring in her ears and of the way her hands felt on the steering wheel of her Jeep as she drove circles through town. These were the pieces of her that she could attach calm to and that could bring her emotions to a level that was manageable. These were the thoughts that ran through her mind as she pictured herself walking into a crowded Manhattan bar and seeing him again, right in front of her. This was the montage that she'd had on repeat for the past week and she did her best to focus on it now.

No matter what happened tonight, she could still call home. She could go for a drive and stop at Dunkin Donuts for a cup of tea, start up a playlist, and just be alone.

No matter what happened tonight, it would end when she walked out of the bar. That was the promise that she would try to keep. There would be nothing further; she would not travel down a road that had already nearly killed her. She simply would not.

Her phone buzzed with a text from Lou, her best friend and the reason for this entire mess. She guessed she'd have to face Max again at some point, just leave it to her best friend to be the driving force. And if Lou was anything, it was a force.

2011
September

"And that was it? You didn't even see him again?" Louisiana Atkins was perched on the far end of Cecelia's dorm bed, cross-legged and devouring a Taylor ham, egg, and cheese on an everything bagel. This was the last step of the routine; every night out was followed by breakfast from their favorite bagel shop, Hole in the Wall, and a thorough examination of anything noteworthy from the night before.

"That was it, Lou. He must've just gone back to the party. And I sure as hell wasn't hanging around in some weird gym uniform. I bolted for the door with my head down," she took a large gulp of her chocolate milk to help a particularly stubborn bit of bagel down her throat. "I'll probably never see him again, this damn school is so big."

"Are you kidding me? We know he hangs out at Theta, we'll just keep going back until we see him again. No biggie, everyone had fun last night anyway so you're not gonna hear arguments from any of the girls," Lou always talked like this, as if she could just decide something and everyone would follow. And, to be fair, she usually did get things done her way.

Louisiana Atkins was the kind of girl Cee had always wished she could be. Singularly beautiful, and in possession of all of the confidence that entailed, Lou's spirit was contagious. She was lively and knew how to ask for exactly what she wanted; Cecelia found Lou's confidence to be the catching kind, since the start of their friendship she was a bit bolder and surer of herself than she'd ever been before.

Lou was vivacious, and more soulful than anyone Cecelia had ever met, which is the reason the two hit it off. There was a balance to their friendship that brought Cee out of her shell and dragged Lou a bit deeper into her own thoughts. It was exactly the kind of friendship Cee had hoped to find when she began her college life, and she was so thankful for the comfort that came with confiding in a friend who always seemed to understand what she was saying even when the words weren't coming out right, even when the words weren't coming out at all.

Cee, and most of the other girls, made it a point to say yes to Lou whenever she came through with an invite. She wanted to experience college life and Lou was laying the foundation for the kind of stuff Cee had seen in the movies. From gathering in boys' dorm rooms to play "Never Have I Ever" to squeezing into mini skirts and dancing at frat parties, Lou had the plans.

Louisiana was named for the home state of her parents, which is where Cee figured a lot of Lou's artistry came from. Her mother was of Creole descent and her father a jazz musician from New Orleans. Cee had met them when they moved Lou into the room next door to Cee's the year before, and again when they'd moved her into the space they now shared – and just in those two brief encounters she could see the energy bouncing off of them in waves.

Lou called her Juice. This charming little nickname came about when Cee went around the dorm and introduced herself to everyone as 'Cecelia, but you can call me Cee,' which prompted too many 'Hi Cee's' for comfort. Lou said she couldn't possibly separate Cecelia from the obnoxious little juice box, so she'd have to just switch it around and call her Juice instead.

Cecelia initially balked at the nickname in no small part due to its not-so-subtle ties to that of one OJ Simpson. She was shushed almost immediately by Lou's insistence that people who kill other people don't get to have nicknames, so Juice was clearly up for grabs. And the day Lou realized she could combine both names and just call her Juicy, well, you would've thought she cracked Da Vinci's code.

"I'm not going to stalk him, Lou! He was cute though, cute and funny. Such a nice combo, ya know?" She took a healthy bite of her sandwich, watching some crumbs land on the paper towel in her lap, and shrugged her shoulders. "It's not every trip to a frat house that you meet someone cute *and* funny. Realistically, it's not every trip to a frat house that we meet someone cute *or* funny," this set both of them laughing.

"Can't disagree with you there, Juice. I managed to have six, count 'em six, separate boys tell me that they saw me in the dining hall yesterday at lunch. You forget to wear a bra *one time*, and all of sudden every guy from here to Timbuktu notices you in the dining hall," Louisiana uncapped her Gatorade bottle and shot Cecelia a mischievous look. "I did give four of them my number though. They showed no signs of it last night, but here's hoping at least one of them is cool."

They leaned across the bed and cheers'd their plastic bottles to that.

CHAPTER 3

2011
September

There weren't many things sweeter than a fall weekend on a college campus, no matter who or where you may be. Maybe it was the fact that the weekend truly was a chance to rest and forget about assignment deadlines and shifts at work and professors who never could just get to the point. Maybe it was the fact that, though it was a time to relax, there were way too many people around for it to ever be boring. Maybe it was just the preconceived notion that weekends were for cherishing, but Cecelia loved nothing more than a Sunday morning at school.

She never wore anything more formal than leggings, she took full advantage of the small TV perched atop a stack of books on her dresser, and she made multiple trips to the dining hall for takeout. On Sundays, lunch was subs, dinner was pasta, and she was damn happy. It was the perfect day.

Of course, it got less fun the later it got. The closer Sunday veered towards Monday morning, the more magic seemed to disappear from this, her favorite day of the week. But she was fully engrossed in her 10 am cup of coffee at the moment and there was really nothing in the whole world that could ruin that for her.

She wandered out to the lounge, leaving a still-sleeping

ONE TIME, BADLY

Louisiana behind, and caught up with some of the other girls. Other than Louisiana, she considered Katie and Shelley to be her closest friends on the floor. Katie was a business major who'd traveled all the way from California to attend Rutgers, while Shelley studied psychology. Cee nestled into a cozy armchair, curled her legs up underneath her, and found her way into the conversation that had apparently been going on for the better part of the morning.

"I just really don't think he should have ratted like that," Katie's own cup of coffee seemed to be the only reason her hands weren't moving in emphasis of her point.

"He was a cop. It was the law. End of story," Shelley wasn't much of a hand-waver to begin with. Her point was made with the calm stare she often shot at anyone trying to disagree with her.

"Yes, I understand that, but it ruined literally everything. It ruined Amanda's life. It ruined Morgan Freeman's life. It even ruined Casey Affleck's own life. It was a bad call."

Oh, so that's what this was about. *Gone Baby Gone* had been shown in the main lounge yesterday afternoon. Clearly, these two had been in attendance.

"Can we please just agree to disagree?" Shelley was done.

"Yeah, of course. I just don't think the world is as black and white as you're trying to make it sound," Katie, it seemed, couldn't help herself from throwing in that last jab.

"Okay, guys. That's probably enough of that," Cee honestly would've loved to join this conversation, but she'd have to take Katie's side and she didn't want to gang up on Shelley. This was not a Sunday conversation. Sunday conversations were far less controversial than this one.

"You're right, Cee. This conversation's gotta go," Katie still seemed a little perturbed at Shelley's "black and white" view of the world via her opinions on a movie that Cecelia honestly couldn't believe neither of them had seen in the three years that it had been out.

"I was thinking of signing up for the volleyball tournament next week. All of the proceeds are going towards breast cancer research. Would you guys want to get a team together? It's only like five bucks," and just like that, Sunday was back on track.

Cecelia got Katie and Shelley on board for the tournament and headed back into her room for a day of absolutely nothing, shaking her head as a faint mention of kidnapping and corruption made its way down the hall.

Cecelia couldn't be late. She had three minutes before Professor Lidrow closed and locked the door of his classroom, leaving her fuming on the outside. This had already happened to her on two occasions, but there was an exam being given today and she'd be damned if her not-so-wonderful punctuality started affecting her grades. She glanced at her watch and picked up the pace, swinging open the door to Historic's Hall and shooting towards the stairs to the second floor.

And it had only been three days, and she hadn't traveled back to the sticky halls of Theta Chi Alpha, but there was Max, turning smack into her, holding a cup of coffee that, it was safe to say, was hotter than piss warm.

"Oh my God! Cecelia! Hey, damn I'm so sorry!"

She was hopping around, waving her arms in front of her, trying to get cool air under her shirt without ripping it off. Max, for his part, seemed to be glued to the spot. His mouth was hanging open, his eyes wide and horrified.

"Hi Max, we really, really, really need to stop meeting like this," the coffee had finally cooled to a bearable temperature and she stopped flailing around so she could readjust her shirt.

"I don't even know what to say to you right now," he ran a bewildered hand through his hair, a wonderful combination of dismay and distress playing across his face. "I kind of want to laugh, but I'm also pretty embarrassed, and I feel *so* bad. That shirt's definitely done for," he gestured towards the milky, caramel colored stain on her white t-shirt. "Please tell me you're leaving class and not on your way in."

"Actually, I have an exam in...3 minutes," she hiked her

bag a little higher on her shoulder, and headed toward the nearby restroom, turning as she went as to not walk with her back to him.

"Which is just enough time to get this off and throw your friend's shirt on. I've had it in my bag in case I ran into you, but it'll have to wait now. I promise though, the next time I see you it's all yours! Bye Max!"

"Just keep it! I should start buying you clothes at this point!" And that was all she heard before the Ladies' Room door swung shut behind her.

2018
September

Four more blocks down and Cecelia was trying her best to let her mind wander. To not obsess to the point of paralysis over this whole thing.

From the moment she'd walked into work that morning, flashing a quick smile at her newly-minted assistant and peeking her head into Stan's office to make sure they were still on for their 10 am regroup, she'd felt her mental fortitude come back to her. She was safe here. She could put her phone in her desk drawer and pretend that the outside world, with all of its worries, didn't exist.

She had enough on her plate at work anyway. She'd nearly groaned out loud as she'd pulled up her calendar for the day. She'd been promoted to Deputy Editor of her department three months prior, and the workload increase had completely overwhelmed her. She'd been promised an assistant from day one, but of course it had taken another six weeks before Human Resources settled on Kevin. He'd proven to be a friendly and efficient asset and Cecelia had been thanking her lucky stars for him every day since.

Skimming through her schedule for the day, she'd realized she'd barely left time for lunch, let alone a meltdown about tonight. But, if she needed just five seconds to catch her breath and calm down, that's what office doors were for. She'd simply click the lock on hers and try to remember who she'd become in the past three years.

She'd remind herself of the good that she'd created all around herself and of the shoulder she'd become for those around her. She'd remember the work that she'd put in to get herself here and focus on the fact that there was no room in her heart or in her mind for regret, she was simply too busy for it.

It was this train of thought that had gotten her through the day, for the most part. It was surreal to think that she'd be seeing him again within the hour. Three years and not a single run-in, but he would definitely be there tonight. Or at least he'd promised Joe that he would swing by. That was unless he'd gotten sick, or hit by a bus (God forbid), or just straight up decided that he wasn't doing this. Because, no matter who you are, this wasn't nothing.

She knew she wasn't being dramatic, she wasn't stressing out about something dumb; this was a big deal. This was something to contemplate and to mentally prepare for. And, for a moment, she wished she would've caved and texted him all those times that she felt so low she could barely keep her eyes open; when her pain was keeping her awake without the energy to move, but without the peace to sleep.

If she'd had just one conversation with him, maybe this wouldn't seem so big to her. Maybe there would be some semblance of closure or comfort between them. Instead, her thoughts of him remained raw and unforgiving – except when they were golden. The sunshine memories were there too. With a small smile, Cecelia turned left and continued on her way.

CHAPTER 4

**2011
October**

Cecelia Scott had loved college from the moment that she'd stepped foot onto the campus on move-in day. She'd enjoyed high school and would definitely miss her friends, but this was what she'd been waiting for.

She'd had this plan all summer to take full advantage of the anonymity she would have here. She'd even debated having people call her CeCe just to really mess with her image, but she honestly hated that name. She didn't want to be known as the girl who cringed every time someone addressed her.

So the name would stay, but she promised herself that very little else would. She wanted to put herself out there and befriend all of the most interesting people living in her dorm. She had her old friends and they would always be there, but this was her chance to meet people that could show her things she'd never been able to learn in the small town that she'd been born and raised in.

The college she'd chosen was said to be one of the most diverse in the country and she was counting on that to be true. She wanted to meet people from different cultures and to have conversations about politics and to study abroad and to do all of the romantic things every girl imagines herself doing when she finally steps a foot out into the real world.

What she hadn't counted on was stepping from one bubble right into another one.

College was tricky that way. Yes, her friends were different. Yes, she was different. But she'd quickly realized that this wasn't what the rest of her life would be like. Nothing could ever be like this again. And it was so good and she was just trying to really take it all in.

Her entire freshman year was spent with eyes wide open, trying to write down every piece of information her professors relayed and trying to say yes to every invitation she got and join every club she saw a flyer for. It was a whirlwind and by the start of her sophomore year she was tired as hell, plain and simple.

So this semester she decided to slow it down. Her schedule was a breeze, she'd knocked it down to one club - a women in communications group that featured different alumni each week - and she was definitely being choosier about the invitations she was accepting (there were some frat houses that were best visited only once).

She'd also gotten into a fairly strict gym routine that she was loving. Running was her new favorite thing and, while she wasn't complaining about the newly toned legs and slimmer waistline, she was more addicted to the feeling she got from it than anything else.

She felt more focused, but more free at the same time. It was incredible. She was sometimes guilty of the crime that all 20-year-old girls fall victim to every once in a while; of imaging themselves as much more basic, and less exquisite, than they truly are and it seemed that a four-mile run was all it took to shake that feeling, at least for a few hours.

Cecelia was feeling balanced in her second year of college. She had settled into a routine, she was knocking down credits and making good grades and she found herself constantly amused by everyone and everything around her. Dull moments were few and far between. Case in point, Louisiana bursting into their room at 8:45 pm on a Wednesday with new plans wasn't so much a surprise as an annoyance.

"Get up, put your books away, we're going out," she was already getting to work on her makeup and pulling the elastic band out of her hair.

"Lou, I'm right in the middle of a hardcore One Tree Hill binge. I need to know if Brooke is actually pregnant or if she's just playing Lucas."

"She's playing him, get up."

"Lou! Come on! That's so messed up."

"Don't care, Juice. We just got invited to Theta for Wine Wednesday. I've been waiting for this. We can't say no."

"Can't you find someone else to go with you? My hair is too greasy."

"It's called dry shampoo. And, no, I can't find someone else. I want my best friend to go with me. And don't you want to find that guy again? Who knows, he might be there."

Cecelia wished that hadn't caught her attention, but it had. Louisiana was right and Cee would be lying if she didn't admit that she'd been hoping to run into Max on her own; something that was unlikely considering the size of their campus. Lou raised her eyebrows as a smile broke out over her face.

"Oooooh I got you there, Juicy. Get your pretty ass up and throw on some pants. We're doing this."

An hour later, Cecelia found herself in jeans and a flowy tank top, hair freshly dry shampooed and pulled into a voluminous ponytail, following Lou out the doors of their dorm building.

After listening to Louisiana chatter on (read: defend herself) about the ethics of spoiling a TV show for a friend in times of great distress for the better part of the past hour, Cecelia found herself in desperate need of a glass of wine, even if it came out of a box.

The scene in the frat house was as expected. A bunch of people milling about, cups in hand. Some groups were making use of the large, black leather sofas set up in the front room while others were leaning on the countertops lining the kitchen walls. It was less crowded than Cecelia had expected, which was nice. At least she had some room to breathe, unlike the last time she'd been here.

Lou weaved her way through the crowd until she found what she'd been looking for. Boxes of bagged wine were lined up along a pop up table in the corner of the kitchen. She filled them each a cup of rosé and turned to Cecelia, a stern expression on her face.

"Now for the real reason we're here," Lou's stare was serious, as was her tone.

"What? What do you mean real reason? I thought we were here to drink wine and then go home," Cecelia could already feel the annoyance seeping into her voice.

"Cee, do you think I'd spoil a very minor plotline on One Tree Hill for a glass of boxed wine?"

"Yeah, Lou. It really wasn't that big of a shock."

"Whatever, that's rude, but it doesn't matter," she looked around conspiratorially, "I'm here for revenge."

"Louisiana?"

"Yeah?"

"I'm leaving."

"Nooo! Cee, please. I'm serious! This is really important," Lou's pleading drew the eyes a few people in their vicinity, but she didn't seem to notice.

"I don't come to Wine Wednesday for revenge. I come to Wine Wednesday for a buzz. I didn't sign up for any craziness tonight."

"It's not going to be crazy. I promise. We just have to stick around long enough for Joe Hemsley to show up and then I do one minor task and we're out. I promise."

"Were we even invited to this party, Lou?"

"No, but that's not important. These people are lucky we're here."

Joe Hemsley turned out to be Louisiana's partner on a history project that she'd been assigned during the first week of classes. As it were, Joe made the mistake of skipping not one, but all three of the scheduled meetings to work on the project, leaving Louisiana to do everything on her own while still getting full credit for his part.

Instead of mentioning it to the professor (which Lou rolled her eyes at as soon as Cee suggested it), Louisiana had decided to get back at Joe in her own, very Louisiana Atkins way.

"I'm going to accuse him of giving me an STD in front of everyone," she honestly looked proud of herself. Cecelia couldn't believe it.

"Lou, that's ridiculous. First off, you're going to tell everyone here that you have an STD, which is just gross. And second, this guy probably won't even care. This is a bad idea."

"I don't care what people in this godforsaken frat house think of me and he will too care. You should see him during class. Leaning over to whisper to any girl that happens to be sitting near him. Passing notes like it's the fucking 4th grade. He lives for the attention. Meanwhile, I'm pulling all nighters trying to write a 30-page report on my own."

"Thirty pages? Screw an STD, tell him you're pregnant."

"That's my girl."

As luck would have it, Joe Hemsley just happened to be standing next to one Max Maylor when Louisiana struck.

"You've got a lot of nerve! I may be cured, but, had you taken the time to respond to any of my texts, you'd know that you, my friend, are not."

This poor guy, he didn't even know what to say. Cecelia could just see his mind working from her spot next to Lou. Trying to place where he knew her from, probably.

"Oh, nothing to say? That's fine. It's on you, buddy. I just wanted to make sure you didn't do this to any other poor, unsuspecting girls on this campus. And to think, I really liked you, Joe. I thought we had something."

And then it clicked.

"Hey, wait, you're in my history class aren't you? You're my partner on that project."

"I was, Joe. I used to be a lot of things that I'm not anymore."

With her cover blown, Lou spun away with a huff of heartbroken frustration and stormed out of the kitchen. Cecelia threw Joe Hemsley a dirty look and was on her way as well when she heard her name called out from behind her.

"Cecelia? Hey, wait up."

It was Max. She had to suppress a smile as he caught up to her in the hallway outside the kitchen.

"Hey, Max. Fancy meeting you here," she stepped to the side to let a group of girls pass by and Max followed suit.

"Listen I'm sorry about your friend. Joe can be an ass sometimes," the look on his face was sincere and Cecelia thought this might not have been the first time that Max found himself mediating a situation that Joe could seemingly care less about.

"Oh, it's okay. No big deal. I actually have to go find her, you know, make sure she's all good." Even though she'd said it, Cecelia made no move to leave.

Max took a quick glance around the room, his eyes landing on something just over Cecelia's shoulder, and smirked.

"Well, it looks like she's doing fine to me."

Cecelia turned around to find Louisiana with a fresh cup of wine in her hands laughing hysterically right alongside good old Joe Hemsley himself.

"I knew it! She was playing him wasn't she?" Max's smile had morphed into something more amused and, if Cee wasn't mistaken, impressed.

"She may or may not have been seeking revenge," Cecelia shot him a smirk as she finished off the wine in her cup.

"Honestly, he really is an ass. I don't blame her. Can I get you another drink?"

"Sure," she gave a small smile and a short nod.

Cecelia followed Max back to the drink table and watched as he peaked into her cup to see what she had been drinking. He promptly picked up the rosé and poured a healthy amount into her cup. She flashed him a smile and took a sip from the top.

"So the white shirt? Done?"

"Done," she laughed. "By the time I got back to my dorm it was too late for intervention."

"I really am sorry," and he had the decency to look genuinely guilty as he said it.

"It was an old shirt anyway. Not a big deal," Cecelia waved it off, she really hadn't cared.

"How'd the exam go? You weren't late?"

"Nope, I made it with a minute to spare."

"Good, good. I was worried," he was smiling now, playful.

"Yeah?"

"Oh yeah. I paced my room for like an hour just praying you made it there," she laughed out loud at that and did a quick scan of the room for Lou, just making sure things were still fine on her front.

When she spotted them again, they were sitting on the couch, talking close. Either Louisiana was in it for the long game with this whole revenge thing or Joe was some kind of magician. She was tempted to go talk to him herself just to see what the fuss was about, but found herself very happily rooted to the spot she was in.

"Looks like Joe and Louisiana are hitting it off," Max shot a glance over his shoulder at her words, nodding his agreement as he turned back to Cecelia.

"Yeah, as bad as he is as with most other stuff, that's how good he is with girls. It's like a gift."

"You should take some lessons. It couldn't hurt," Cecelia made a show of raising her eyebrows and taking a long sip of wine.

His mouth was hanging open when she peered back over her cup.

"Take that back."

"I can't. You have two strikes with me and we've only met twice. You're average is not good, Max."

"Or is my average amazing?"

"I don't follow."

"Well, you're here talking to me right? I was just setting

myself apart. Anyone can feed you lines, but can they really ingrain themselves in your memory?" Cecelia did her best not to laugh out loud at that.

"Please don't tell me you spilled two separate beverages on me on two separate occasions to 'set yourself apart'."

"No, I'm not that dumb, but it's something to think about."

"What?" It was more an exclamation than a question.

"Just weird that it keeps happening," he held his hands up, as if to say that he didn't have any part of it, it was out of his control.

"Yeah, I mean it's definitely not normal."

"It's like our thing."

"Oh god, don't say that. I'm going to start walking around with a rain coat on."

"Well, definitely don't do that," a bit of the playfulness had left his tone. He looked at her with a different gleam in his eye now.

"No?"

"No, this is a much better look."

"So I have a confession to make," she could feel herself starting to blush under his gaze and she didn't want him to catch her slipping.

"And what's that," he was all ears now, just waiting for what she was about to say.

"I only really came tonight because I thought you might be here," she made sure to meet his eyes when she said it.

"It wasn't for the show your buddy just put on?" He was smiling at her, a false air of skepticism playing across his features.

"No, that was a bonus. I didn't know she was going to do that until we were already here."

"Well, while we're being honest, I might have been at every single party these animals have thrown in the past three weeks looking for you."

"FOMO on Cecelia?" she guessed.

"FOMO on Cecelia for real."
"Maybe you should take my number so it doesn't happen again?"

CHAPTER 5

**2011
October**

The amount of time that it took for Max Maylor to use her phone number was unacceptable. Some (read: Cecelia) might even call it cruel. She'd anxiously stared at her phone for days, her heart jumping at every message that came in, and then plummeting when it wasn't him. She hadn't had a crush like this since Tommy Chambers in her junior year of high school; that one hadn't really gone her way either.

But Max had seemed so interested! He'd spent that whole party talking to only her. He'd flirted and leaned in close and Louisiana even agreed that it was messed up for him to not even attempt to communicate with her. Joe Hemsley had texted Lou the very next day. Even that asshat had pulled it together.

So, when she finally heard from Max again nearly two weeks later, it was with the utmost contempt that she unlocked her phone and opened the message. He'd missed his window, she'd officially left the giddy little bubble she'd been in when she'd walked out the door of Theta that night and returned to normal girl status, no heart-shaped eyes here.

Free tonight?

So he'd spent the past two weeks thinking of the dumbest, most vague text he could send and landed on this. Fantastic.

She waited a good 40 minutes before answering, no need

to rush on his account. Cecelia was safely tucked away in her 1 pm class when she typed back.

Maybe. What's up?

She was committing to nothing without the details.

Wine Wednesday at my place. Come! Bring your crazy friend

Damn. She loved Wine Wednesday. She shot Lou a quick text just confirming that she was free before she thought too much about her response. She definitely wasn't going alone, so if Lou had plans she'd have to just tell Max she'd see him another time. At least she had his number now.

Louisiana, of course, was always free for Wine Wednesday. She shouldn't have even bothered asking.

Instead of answering, Cecelia dropped her phone into her bag and zipped it up. She'd respond after class and let him know that she and her crazy friend would be there.

Until then, there were notes to be taken and outfit options to mentally sift through.

When Cecelia and Louisiana walked into Max's house that night, it was with the most casually cute outfits they could muster. They'd both agreed that the last minute invite was weak and the effort put in must be minimal.

For her part, Cecelia was in a pair of skinny jeans with her gray converse sneakers and a white v-neck t-shirt. Her long chestnut hair still held a light wave from when she'd curled it that morning before class and she'd settled for just a bit of blush and lip gloss to compliment the mascara she always wore.

Louisiana had opted for a long-sleeved dress and a pair of knee-high boots.

"I thought we were going super casual? That outfit is semi-casual at best!" Cecelia complained as she and Louisiana locked up their dorm and walked towards the elevators.

"Cee, there's only a few weeks left to let the legs out before they freeze, I'm taking advantage," she'd explained with a shrug of her shoulders.

Cecelia took this as confirmation that Joe would also be attending this particular event.

The house had the telltale signs that only inhabitants of the male persuasion leave behind. Holes in the walls, raunchy posters strewn about and a film of what was hopefully beer on every inch of the hardwood floors. Cecelia could feel the soles of her shoes sticking for just a second with each step she took.

Lou immediately spotted a few friends from class and dragged Cee over to mingle with them. She spent the next fifteen minutes nodding halfheartedly as the group ragged on their shared professor while shooting vague glances around the room, looking for the person at this party that she knew.

When Lou finally excused herself from the conversation, the two headed to the kitchen to grab a drink. It was there that Max Maylor was holding court. He was perched on the counter top, drink in hand, telling what seemed to be the most hilarious story ever told. That's if the insane giggling from the group of girls in front of him was anything to go by.

Great. She came all this way just to watch Max hit on random girls while Lou greeted acquaintances and old friends alike as if she were the mayor of College Avenue. Cecelia seemed to go unnoticed as she and Lou filled up their solo cups with watery beer from the keg in the corner of the room. She was trying her best not to look Max's way, leaving it to him to break away from the group to greet her. She wasn't about to push her way through just to say hello.

Louisiana was quietly shooting nervous glances at Cee, clearly wondering if they should hang around or grab their drinks and keep on moving. The second Lou handed her cup to her, Cecelia headed for the door leading out of the room. She caught Max's glassy eyes as she walked out of the kitchen and his story faltered for a second, distracted. And then she continued on her way.

"Well, that was kind of weird. I thought he would wave you over or something," Lou sipped from the top of her drink, trying her best to avoid the layer of foam that had yet to dissolve.

"Yeah, I know. Awkward."

"Let's just drink our drinks. I'm sure he'll come find you in a minute," she said it with only the confidence that Lou could lend to completely unlikely scenarios. Still, Cecelia wanted to give him a chance to come talk to her. Now that he knew she was here, the ball was in his court.

"Yeah, hopefully," she took a large gulp of her beer, turning to follow Louisiana into the crowd.

She wasn't surprised that Lou knew so many people here; she seemed to make friends everywhere she went. Cee's reserve left her with acquaintances to wave to and smile at, shoot a quick 'How are you?' and a 'Good seeing you' here and there, but no one to really catch up with. These nights always left her wondering how much time Lou actually spent paying attention in class if she walked out with this many new friends.

Her phone buzzed with a goodnight text from her mom, which came in at around 10:30 pm each and every night. *Night, sweetie. Love you.* It always made her smile when she saw the message, even though she knew it was coming.

She typed back a quick *Love you, too! Goodnight!* and turned to find the bathroom and maybe get a refill. That first drink went quickly, but it's not like there was much else to do at this place.

When she returned to the kitchen, Max was in the same spot, but there was just one girl with him now, standing between his legs with her hands resting on his thighs. His hands were cupping her face, his head bent towards hers in a way that could only mean one thing. She could just make out the working of his jaw from her angle. This was bullshit.

Cecelia put her cup down on the counter and stalked out of the room, tracking down Lou, grabbing her drink out of her hands and pulling her right out the front door.

"What the hell is going on?"

"I don't even understand why he asked me to come!" she downed the remnants of Lou's drink and tossed the cup. It landed somewhere on the porch that circled Max's house. Good. Let him clean it up. "Ridiculous!"

"Cee, what happened?" Lou was half-jogging beside Cee as if she couldn't keep up. All drama, all the time.

"He was making out with some skank in the kitchen." The words came out more forcefully than she'd intended them to, but she was worked up. A proper storming out could do that.

"No!" Lou was scandalized.

"Yes!" Cee was pissed off.

"Why even invite me to this bullshit party if he wasn't even going to bother acknowledging me? I don't get it."

"That dick. Let me go back in. I'll spill a quick drink on them and be out in under a minute," Lou made to move back towards the house, but Cecelia grabbed her arm. The anger was seeping from her with each step away from the party, turning to something much worse.

"It's really not worth it. It's not like we're together or anything. Maybe I read this whole thing wrong and he was just trying to be nice inviting me tonight," her voice had grown very small now, logic interfering with emotion.

"Cee, boys don't just do things to be nice. He was flirting with you last time you saw each other and then he invites you to a party at his place. You didn't read anything wrong, maybe he's just an asshole and he went for the first girl that walked in tonight."

"Yeah, he probably asked a bunch of girls to come and I showed up too late," she hated that the disappointment of the night now felt more like her own fault than his.

"Oh well, better to find out now than when you actually like him."

"I kind of did actually like him, though. This is so annoying," she groaned, because what else could she do now.

"Come on, Cee. Let's stop at the student center and grab some Ben & Jerry's. We can just download a movie. As it were, Joe blew me off tonight so he could 'study' and it's honestly the least believable thing another human being has ever said to me."

With that, Lou and Cecelia headed off towards better things. Ice cream and TV boyfriends hadn't managed to let them down a single time.

Before Cecelia knew it, Halloween was fast approaching and that meant just a few weeks before the semester started to wind down and she'd be heading home for an entire month.

Cecelia was going as the four seasons along with Lou and two of the other girls from their floor. She'd lucked out and gotten winter in their random drawing and she was planning on "frosting" her hair and eyelashes and picking up some tulle and white glitter from the craft store to make her own snowy costume.

She had a white skater dress she didn't mind sacrificing for the cause and she planned on wearing over the knee socks and her cute quilted snow boots to tone it down a bit.

Lou would be donning an array of colorful leaves as fall, while Katie and Shelly would be going as summer and spring, respectively.

Normally she'd have another outfit prepared for Saturday night, but she was planning on going home for the weekend to watch her younger sister Sedona's soccer game. She would be playing her rival school and, as it was her senior year, Sedona was freaking out about beating them one last time. Cee didn't want to miss it.

She hadn't heard from Max since the party and, from the way he was going to town on that chick, she didn't expect to. Whatever. She was about to be caught up in the whirlwind that is the end of fall semester, she'd probably forget all about him by the time Santa Claus made his way to New Jersey.

One of her coworkers, a sweet girl named Gwen, had invited the whole front desk crew to a bonfire at her place tonight and Cee figured it wouldn't hurt to ditch the girls from her dorm for once and meet some new people. Also, it was sacrilegious to turn down a bonfire invitation at the end of October. Just wasn't something a girl could do.

So she bundled up in her coziest oversized sweater, threw on a pair of skinny jeans and camel colored over the knee boots and spent the night mingling with a whole new crew. Gwen was a bio major and her friends were smart in a totally different way than Cee's usual group. They read different books and watched different TV shows and it turned out to be a really fun night.

It was the kind of night that acts as a refresher of sorts, a reminder that the world is big and the person sitting next to you on the bus or in the classroom has a story so different from your own.

By the time Cee donned her shimmery, snowflake costume, all thoughts of a blue-eyed boy with the habit of spilling drinks of all kinds were slipping from her mind.

2018
September

Her shoes had officially transitioned from uncomfortable to painful, but it would have to be ignored. Maybe it would be good to have a distraction from what was about to happen. Maybe she'd be able to forget about the butterflies in her stomach and the pounding of her heart once the leather of her shoe finally took a layer of skin off her ankle.

Her first meeting of the day, the 10:30 that she and Stan had met and prepared for, had gone exceptionally well and that high had followed her for hours. They'd pitched a new series for the site to publish; it would be a short weekly advice column featuring a different employee each week.

It was something she and Stan had been talking about for months and they'd finally settled on a format that they thought would work for the site. Cee was excited to see the different responses that came in from her own peers as well as the older members of the staff. There was a definite possibility that it could come off as stale and tank, but she felt optimistic about it and was grateful that the rest of the team had agreed to give it a shot.

It was just the kind of personal victory that she needed today and she made sure to let herself bask in it for as long as possible. She always felt this sense of power after a successful meeting, especially one where she'd done the bulk of the presenting. It took a lot to walk into a room, especially one filled with her superiors, and own it.

While Cee had always been comfortable with public speaking and had even found herself enjoying presentations during her school years, this was a different ballgame entirely. It was something she'd struggled with at the beginning of her career, but, like so many things, had become second nature to her now.

The win had also given her something to look forward to. She enjoyed her job and felt fulfilled by it on some level each day, but there was nothing like starting a new project. She loved the feeling of creating something from scratch and working out the kinks as she went along. She was already assembling a list of the first few colleagues she planned on interviewing and she couldn't wait to get started.

For a little while, it took her past the night ahead of her and into a future where she was doing what she did best.

The crowds started to slim down the further uptown she went. It was amazing the difference just a few blocks could make in the city. One moment you're smack in the middle of a swarm of people, and the next you're looking over your shoulder to make sure you're not too alone on a block you're not familiar with.

Although, getting mugged would do her one better than a distraction; it would be an excuse to just blow the whole night off.

CHAPTER 6

**2011
December**

It was a breezy mid-December morning when she saw him again. He hadn't noticed her, and she was hesitant to grab his attention. She didn't necessarily want to talk to him, but the crumbled up t-shirt in the bottom of her backpack was a constant reminder that they had some form of unfinished business. Had the shirt been Max's she wouldn't have cared, but she felt bad keeping a shirt that belonged to someone that she hadn't even met. What if he really liked it?

She assessed the situation. Max Maylor, seven feet away, no beverage in sight. It was safe to approach. She'd just hand him the shirt and be on her way. No need for any conversation. She turned on her heel and headed in his direction.

He seemed to be tuned out of the present moment, failing to notice her until she'd said his name twice. He looked up at her and a slow smile spread across his face, as if she'd just caught him waking up from a nap rather than at midday in the middle of the quad.

"Hey," was all he offered. There wasn't an ounce of guilt or awkwardness to it. If anything, he looked as if running into her was the best thing that could've happened to him in that very moment. There was note of excited anticipation in his tone, as if the whole Wine Wednesday debacle hadn't happened at all.

"Um, hey Max. I just wanted to finally return your friend's stuff," she retrieved it from the bottom of her bag, trying to straighten it out a bit before she handed it to him. "And just as a side note, if you have a drink in your hand the next time I see you, I'm keeping a five-foot distance."

"Five feet? You're underestimating both my arm strength and the physical matter of all liquids," he made no move to grab the shirt from her outstretched hands, his quick response doing nothing to shake the mellow vibe he was giving off.

"Are you okay? You seem dazed or, I don't know, something's off."

"All nighter, and I just spent the past two hours slowly dying in my exam. And fall is definitely over, so that sucks too. I hate when fall is over," he was rambling now, but it wasn't the nervous kind.

It was almost as if he forgot she was there and he was just thinking out loud. She saw him catch himself and meet her eyes again. "I was actually going to grab lunch, any chance you want to save this day from being the actual worst day of my college career?"

"Really? Did you not hear the whole five feet from you and drinks thing?" She was gearing up to say no. A snide comment about the last time he'd invited her somewhere was on the tip of her tongue. But it wasn't worth it. The few weeks since she'd seen him had cooled her initial sadness at their last encounter. Facts were facts; she didn't know him and he didn't owe her anything. Maybe getting lunch with him might not be the worst thing in the world.

"We can take this time to draw up the legal documents. 'I, Max Maylor, promise to resist approaching Cecelia Something while holding any beverage, hot or cold'," he laughed lightly. He gestured vaguely in the direction of the dining hall, a quirk to his brow. "I promise not to spill anything on you in the meantime, and I might even swipe you in."

"You don't have to swipe me in," she said in answer to his original question. "And I won't be signing any legal documents without a lawyer present."

He let out an easy laugh at that as she fell into step with him and she felt her shoulders begin to relax. It was one meal, no big deal.

She'd never seen someone more successfully take advantage of Rutgers' meal plan than Max Maylor. He seemed to have breakfast, lunch, and dinner on his tray within five minutes, and he couldn't stop talking about the ice cream he was going to eat when he was done. For her part, Cecelia had a respectable cheeseburger and fries combo, and was considering grabbing some pasta salad to go with it.

"The way I see it, we have to take advantage of the buffet. We're paying for it, and I for one don't like wasting money. I like to feel like I'm beating the system," he led her to a table on the outer edge of the dining hall, pulling out a seat for her with one hand and sliding into his own in one smooth motion.

"There's beating the system, and then there's eating to the point of explosion. At this point I'm not even worried about you spilling your drink, I think you might actually projectile vomit on me if you eat all that," Cecelia took a bite of her burger and tried not to laugh as Max's eyebrows rose up at the image she'd just painted.

"Yeah, this is definitely excessive. But, like I said, I had a terrible night and an even worse morning so I'm going to comfort eat my way through the afternoon."

"Fair enough. So what was this soul sucking exam on?"

"Some advanced calculus class. I don't even want to talk about it, I think I'm going to have to change my major after this one," he seemed genuinely heavy-hearted about it.

"I'm sure you did better than you think, especially if you spent the whole night reviewing everything."

"I guess we'll see, nothing I can do about it now."

"That's the spirit! Admit defeat and eat a seven course meal at 1 pm. That'll do the trick."

"If you keep talking about how much food I'm about to house, I'm gonna get a complex, Cecelia."

"Okay, okay I'm sorry. No more talk of food or exams."

"Awesome. Thank you, much appreciated," he sent her a wink and a smile as he bit into some gauzy pastry.

"No problem, I think the agreement was that I save this day from being the worst of your college career, not tank it even more."

"Yes, I love a woman that sticks to a deal, very good quality."

"Would you like to talk about what seems to be an insurmountable tendency to spill any drink that finds its way into your hands?"

"I swear that you're the only person that I've ever spilt a drink on in my life! And for it to happen twice, I can't even explain it. But I have to say, and you're not gonna like it, but I have to say you definitely get an assist on the history building incident," he held up his hands as if to say there was nothing he could do about it, facts are facts.

"What?! You doused me in scalding coffee. I definitely didn't *assist* you in that!" Cecelia put her burger back on the plate for this one.

"You ran right into me! And 'scalding' is a little dramatic, that coffee was lukewarm at best before I lost it to your shirt."

"*Lost* it to my shirt? I'm going to forfeit this conversation for the sole purpose of having it end in you describing what happened as you *losing* your coffee to my shirt."

"Okay, but I would just like to say, and we can consider this the start of a new conversation, that I am a very coordinated person. Some people might even call me 'Athlete of the Month'."

"Oh yeah? And where are these fanatical Max Maylor fans located?"

"That would be Lyndhurst, New Jersey. Born and bred."

"You're not from Lyndhurst."

"You got something against Lyndhurst? I'll have you know it's a fantastic town, great parks, great restaurants. Home of the Maylor family for four generations."

"Very nice description. If I'd never been, I'd most definitely want to visit. But I have been to Lyndhurst, many times actually. I'm from Nutley."

"No way! What a small world! We grew up ten minutes from each other, and it took me ruining your day twice for us to actually meet? You gotta love it, we're like those people that grow up down the street from each other in some small European town only to meet half way around the world."

"Such a coincidence! You just took that so far with the whole Europe thing, but it really is crazy."

"Any analogy is a good analogy! What's your last name, do you have any siblings I would know from sports or something like that?"

"It's Scott, Cecelia Scott. I have a younger sister named Sedona, we both played soccer all through high school. I guess we never would've crossed paths."

"I guess not. I did football and hockey. I have a younger sister, Isabella, but she isn't into sports. She's a really good painter, you should see her stuff, I think she could start selling it and she's only 18 years old."

"That's cool, good for her! I always wished I could paint, but I'm like one level above stick figures when it comes to art."

"Same, she got all the good genes, she's smarter than me too."

"You're a good brother, I don't even have to see you with her to know. You're all smiley and proud when you talk about her. It's sweet."

"Good timing, I just started considering sweet a compliment. It used to make me cringe, but now I see it for what it really is."

"What is it really?"

"Well, it's you saying you like me."

"Whoa, what? That's not what I said," Cecelia was doing her best to keep up with the quick turn their conversation had taken. What the hell?

"I think it might've been what you meant, though," the

ONE TIME, BADLY

fact that he was smiling at her, clearly pleased that he'd knocked her off her guard, was not helping things. She felt herself blink once, twice.

"You're kind of crazy, has anyone ever told you that before?" Cecelia popped a fry into her mouth to slow down the pace of the conversation. She took a second to chew and swallow. "I don't like you. I don't even know you."

"You might like me though, if I hadn't acted like such a jackass the last time we saw one another," he was watching her closely, trying to gauge her reaction to this topic of conversation.

"*That* I'll agree with," Cecelia met his gaze.

"I've been wanting to apologize to you for that, but I figured a text would just seem dumb at this point. I saw you in the kitchen for a second and I looked for you later on, but I was pretty messed up pretty early on and I guess you'd left by that point."

"It's all right. It's not like you owed me anything. I'm not going to deny that I went to the party hoping to see you, but you were hosting so I shouldn't have expected you to be able to just ignore everyone else for me."

"I know I didn't owe you anything, but I invited you there so that we could hang out. All I'm saying is that I'd be pissed if you invited me to a party and didn't even bother to say hi to me. That's my bad and I'm sorry for it. But I don't want it to seem like I just blew you off. I knew I messed up at the party and I didn't really know what to say so I just dropped it, which obviously didn't help anything either," He was clearly still not quite sure how to handle the conversation, if his rambling was any indication.

"Max, please. This is totally unnecessary. It's really fine," she was trying her best to make her voice sound light, but the whole thing was making her feel as awkward as she'd felt the night it happened.

"What I really want to say is that I've been thinking about you. I was honestly just kidding about the whole 'FOMO on Cecelia' thing at first, but I've been feeling it for the past few weeks and I'm happy that we ran into one another. And thank you for coming to lunch with me," he nodded his head in conclusion. He'd said what he'd meant to say, that was that.

"Okay, if we're being *this* honest then I have to say that I was really bummed about the party. I even littered on your porch on my way out, it was that bad," she lifted her shoulders and let them drop back down.

"Wait, are you saying that you left about eighty disgusting solo cups on the front porch? That was you? Damn, you really were pissed off," he shook his head, taking another bite of his donut.

"Max," she groaned. "Don't make fun of me! What happened to the nice apology that you were in the middle of?"

"My long-winded apology is officially over. Do you accept it?"

"I do. It wasn't necessary, but I appreciate it."

"Cool. If it makes you feel any better, I made an ass of myself. I walked straight into a wall at the end of the night and bit through my lip. It was one of the dumbest things I've ever done and I got blood everywhere."

"Wish I could've seen it, Max. I really do."

"You would've loved it. I woke up with a fat lip and I ruined my favorite shirt. I wore it just for you and now it's in the garbage."

"Please don't complain about ruined clothes to me, Max."

"Heard and understood, Cecelia. Heard and understood."

Max called her that night, to the absolute shock of every other girl in the study lounge. They'd all had different work to get done, so they'd grabbed their headphones and some communal snacks and headed to the main floor of their building, where the nicest lounge was located.

With new chairs and ample outlets, it was by far the best place to get homework done except for the library, which Cecelia reserved for emergencies only. Lou and a few of their other friends would often head there to get away from the dis-

ONE TIME, BADLY

tractions of their dorm building, but everyone knew that if Cee showed up she was most likely drowning in some type of workload crisis.

When her phone began vibrating from where it sat next to her Macbook on the swing-around desk attached to her chair, Max's name clearly displayed, they all looked at one another with eyebrows raised. Cecelia's hand hovered over the phone for a split second, her nerves getting the best of her.

"A phone call, Cee? Better watch out, he might not know how to spell," Lou joked and the others burst out laughing.

Cecelia shot them a look and accepted the call as she hopped out of the chair and walked through the doors to sit on a bench outside.

"You just shook every single one of my friends to their core with this call," Cecelia said by way of hello.

"Oh yeah? What about you? Feeling shook in any way, shape, or form?"

"Nah, I'm good. Believe it or not, I can speak. Although it has been called into question whether or not you can spell."

She could hear him let out a laugh on the other end of the line and she smiled at that. There was such an ease between them. She hated those nervous first few weeks in the beginning of most relationships, but they were just chugging right along. She credited the ridiculousness of their previous meetings for that. There was really nowhere to go but up from there.

"So, what are you up to?" Max said as his laughter died away.

"Just getting some work done, thinking I might want to get started on an essay I have due at the end of the week."

"Ah, I'm glad you brought that up. I was going to ask you about your end of the week plans."

"Weekend plans? Not much, probably just going out with the girls. My friend Lou mentioned heading to Theta again maybe."

"I gotta give it to you, Cecelia. You stay one step ahead of me. I've been trying to catch up to you and it's just not going my way."

"Ah, but I can't seem to outrun whichever drink you've chosen to enjoy at a given moment."

"Touché, low blow, but touché."

"So you're going to Theta, too."

"I am."

"Well, then I guess I'll see you there."

"You most definitely will. That FOMO on Cecelia thing just keeps getting worse."

"Glad to hear it, Max. I have to get back inside, but I'll talk to you later?"

"You can expect a text with really big, hard to spell words and all I ask is that you show it to whom it may concern."

"Goodnight, Max." she said with a laugh.

"Night, Cecelia."

By the time Friday rolled around, Cecelia was desperate for a night out. She'd put that essay off until the last minute and had ended up forfeiting half of her night's sleep drawing comparisons between the representation of 'tomb' and 'womb' in Toni Morrison's 'Beloved'. She tended to work well under pressure and was happy with the final product when she reread it this morning, but she just wished she could put up a better fight against her tendency towards procrastination once in a while. She'd then had two classes and a shift at her part-time job at the visitor center to struggle through. Her exhaustion had somehow worn off, leaving her wired.

Max texted her around 8 pm, making sure she was still planning on coming to the party and she felt a wave of excitement run up her spine. She gave it a second, then texted back that she'd be there around 10 pm. This gave her and the girls a chance to get dressed and have a few drinks at the dorm before heading to the frat house. She so wished she was able to just throw on a pair of jeans and sneakers and head to a dive bar, but she was eight months away from that wonderful bit of freedom.

She tried to focus on the fun aspects – free drinks, no bartenders to flag down - rather than the downsides. It was this thought that was interrupted by Lou bursting into their shared dorm room, a discreet coffee cup in hand, which judging by the look on her face, was most definitely not holding coffee.

"Cee! It's your big night!" Lou squealed as she began rummaging around her closet, pulling a satin shirt off of one hanger and unclipping a patterned skirt from another one. She began to change into her outfit as Cecelia started on her own makeup, having already decided on what to wear.

"Oh come on, Lou. It's no big deal." Cecelia smirked at herself in the mirror as she waited for Lou's reaction.

"Don't you *dare*! I'm living vicariously through you tonight, don't play it like you're not even a little bit excited."

"I'm totally kidding. He just texted me and I almost threw up. Get your straightener out, I need you to do my hair."

And with that, Lou let out a scream and rushed to get her "hair station" ready for her best friend.

Cecelia walked into the frat house with a bounce in her step and her favorite mini dress on. She'd texted Max to let him know she was on her way, and he'd told her to meet him in the kitchen when she got there. Apparently he was wrapped up in an intense game of flip cup and he couldn't get away to meet her at the door. The fact that he'd even thought to escort her into the party was enough for her. This was college after all; she wasn't expecting to be drowning in chivalry.

The second she walked into the kitchen and met Max's eyes, she knew she was in deep, deep trouble.

He was wearing one of those quarter-length sleeved baseball style shirts that should've come off as boyish, but always just looked hot instead, paired with jeans that fit like he'd had them tailored to his frame and the same sneakers he'd had on the night that they'd met. He'd clearly been running his hand back through his hair. She was willing to bet it was the result of the aforementioned stressful game of flip cup and she was so thankful to whoever had invited him to play.

He smiled at her like she'd walked in carrying a birthday cake in one hand and a million dollars in the other and she was just so sold. All she wanted to do was kiss him, right there in the middle of the packed kitchen, but she just stood there in the doorway as her friends began complaining behind her. *Why'd you stop? Do you see him? Is someone in your way, move them!*

Max's smile only grew as he turned away from the beer-drenched table and walked across the room towards her. He didn't stop when he reached her, instead he grabbed her head in his hands and laid one on her that, to this day, she couldn't shake.

2018
September

Just the memory of that first real kiss between them had her shivering now, at 26 years old on a busy New York City street. It was the feeling in her gut when he stepped back from her, that smile on his face taking a lazier look, that had her convinced that this man would mean something more to her than she'd felt before. And she was right, she was so right in that moment. He was more than more had ever been before.

It struck her as odd, she remembers, the immediate connection that she'd felt to him. She'd never had that before, never so strong, and never so quick. She wasn't just thinking about him. She was losing time going over the things he said, and the way he said them. And she couldn't wait to hear what he'd come up with next.

He was so different than anyone she'd ever met before, and so very different from the person she'd expected him to be when she followed him through the crowded halls of a frat house she would've forgotten years ago had it not flashed before her eyes a million times. Whenever she thought of seeing him for the first time. Whenever she thought of all of the signs she'd missed along the way.

She remembers the guilt of knowing deep down that she wasn't doing a good job making time for her friends, but Max was new and she was obsessed in that way that makes a person forget certain things, like who they were before. But, just like she knew it wasn't right, she also knew that her friends would understand. Because they'd all been there, and it doesn't stay that way. The balance comes with a little bit of time.

It's like your world revolves around him they would say, wearing the same accusatory looks on their faces. She knew she was supposed to deny it immediately, she was supposed to claim that she still had the same priorities as before she'd let him swipe her into the over-crowded dining hall and watched him eat more food than could've possibly been healthy. But, that wasn't the truth.

She found no reason to be ashamed that she'd opened her heart so completely. He'd made her so uniquely happy that she wasn't sure how not to hold him dear. The way she saw it, her world wasn't revolving around him, but around a distinct bliss that he happened to be holding in his outstretched hands.

It was the feeling he gave her, of being so strong and happy that it couldn't possibly ever fade. Even just the memory of it would be enough to go off of forever. And she felt that she might be the first person in the history of the world to live forever. Or maybe there was a secret society of immortals that walked among us and she was about to find out that she belonged to it. That was the way he made her feel.

To this day, she'd tell you the one thing that set Max apart from any other sorta-maybe-boyfriend was his ease in courting her. He didn't seem to question the trajectory of their relationship; he went with the flow, making everything feel like the natural next step. Sometimes he pushed them forward, like the kiss in the kitchen of that party, completely out of the blue. And it felt natural, and from then on when they hung out there was always a little bit of kissing involved. And, because she had no experience with any of this, she let him set the pace.

He took her cues and slowed down when she started getting nervous, and was happy to sit back and let her take the lead once her confidence grew. His ease put her at ease, his confidence made her bolder. She would always be grateful for that.

The way he taught her to be confident in this way without ever pointing out that it was something she was lacking.

She was in love with him by January. Completely besotted, and completely unashamed. As far as Cecelia was concerned, there was no luckier girl on the planet than the one that got Max Maylor. And it was her, and she was trying to be cool about it, but sometimes all she could think to say was *your face is my favorite face, your hands are my favorite hands, your arms are my favorite arms. Is there any* thing *about me that's your favorite thing? Are* my *hands your favorite hands?*

Cecelia and Max existed blissfully in the bubble that is college all the way through graduation. And the bubble was beautiful, and the bubble was pure magic, and then the bubble burst.

She felt her phone buzz in the pocket of her jacket, signaling a new text message. It was probably from Lou, asking why she was late. She'd told her she'd be there around 7 pm, but her choice to walk had held her up and she found that she was already fifteen minutes late. Normally, Lou wouldn't have cared or probably even noticed, but she knew her friend was probably nervous that she'd bail at the last minute.

Instead, the message read only two words. *He's here.*

And with that, Cecelia shook the shiver from her spine and let her steps falter. She took a second, squared her shoulders and began to walk again. He was there, and soon, she would be too.

CHAPTER 7

2012
January – May

There is a certain variety of happiness that translates to pure energy. It's a form of adrenaline and there's got to be a scientific explanation for this; some mix of chemicals that breathes life into your body, endorphins raging through your system. Either way, it's addictive. It makes everything brighter, it makes everything easier.

Max seemed to have too much energy for his own body now. He was always fidgeting; he could never sit still. It was as if his body just couldn't contain all that was going on inside of it. Sometimes Cecelia would watch him, his hands in constant motion, drumming on the table in front of him or running through his hair, and wonder if some of that was her affect on him. She really hoped so.

She credited him for the extra mile per day she was running, for the schoolwork that was getting done even though she was barely getting four hours of sleep a night. It just all seemed very possible to her. She wasn't even tired. And, when she did sleep, there was no tossing or turning. It was pure, sleep-of-the-dead magic and it was doing her a world of good.

She made it to work on time, she made it to class almost on time, and she especially made it to Max on time. The house he shared with six of his buddies was disgusting to say the least.

Like, should-be-condemned levels of grossness. Dirty dishes and layers of dust didn't even begin to cover the damage of this place. She tried not to look around when she walked through.

Max's room, which he shared with a nice enough kid named Adam, was decently clean. At least it smelled nice, despite the piles of laundry everywhere. For the most part, this is where they hung out. It wasn't any more private than her place, but it somehow seemed like it was because it was technically off campus.

But, with Louisiana away for the night and the chance to have a room with a bed all to themselves with no roommate just feet away, it was her dorm that they were in tonight. Max had gotten out of class late and showed up at her door around 10 pm, take away in hand.

"Sorry, the professor honestly wouldn't stop talking. He ran an extra 20 minutes for absolutely no reason," if the look on his face was any indication, that hadn't been the only thing to go wrong for him throughout the day. He looked beat.

He popped a quick kiss on her mouth as he entered the room and tossed the bag in his hand on her desk as he made his way over to the bed.

"Don't you want to eat that?"

"I already had two burgers on my walk over, that's just some extra fries if you want them," he was already sprawled face down on her bed, shoes kicked off haphazardly along the way.

"I'm good."

"Well, then come on over here. I missed you today," he rolled onto his back and propped himself up against her headboard. It was the coziest that her dorm bed had looked in ages.

She crossed the room to him, crawling onto his lap and kissing him hard on the mouth.

"I missed you, too."

"Mm? Tell me about it," it was a whisper against her mouth.

Cecelia threaded her fingers through his and kissed him again.

"I missed your hands."

She let him go and reached for the hem of his shirt, dragging it over his head and tossing it to the side. She nuzzled into the warmth of his neck, taking a deep breath and letting it out against him.

"I missed the way you smell."

This earned her a soft laugh as she went for his mouth again, this time taking advantage of the opening he left her.

"I missed the way you taste."

Her hands were moving south now and he knew well enough to stretch out along the bed, giving her the access she was asking for. She helped him rid himself off his sweatpants and left a lingering kiss on his mouth.

Then she was kissing her way down his chest and he threaded his fingers through her hair. She loved him like this. All sensation; no quick comments. When she took him in her mouth she felt real power course through her body. It was perfect.

When she'd finished and crawled her way back up his body, she felt the confidence coming off of her in waves. No matter how many times she'd done this for him, it still felt like a power move each and every time. It was something so simple, but it was the basis of so much more.

She waited for his breathing to even out before she took her own shirt off and climbed back on top of him.

"No, no, no. Your turn, Cee."

And with that, he flipped her over so she was on her back, his frame braced on strong arms just above her.

She unbuttoned her jeans and he dragged them down her legs, slowly pulling the fabric off of her calves and kissing his way back up the skin he'd just exposed.

She could see the glimmer in his eyes as he neared her center and she let out a small moan of anticipation. As much as she loved him as he'd been just minutes ago, she loved him even more like this.

His rough fingers looped through the lace of her underwear and the door behind them swung open. Louisiana stopped dead in her tracks.

"Shit! Shit. I'm so sorry. I must have eaten something bad, I threw up at the freaking camp out and they made me come home. But I really need a shower so you guys just please keep going and I'll be back in an hour. I'm so sorry!" Lou's mad rambling hadn't even allowed Cecelia to get a word in, but what would she even had said?

Both she and Max had remained deadly still as Louisiana rushed out of the room, shower supplies in hand. Once the door was shut behind her, Max let his head drop to rest on Cecelia's hip, his hair tickling her stomach.

"Well, shit. That really killed the mood, didn't it?"

"Poor Lou, that's so embarrassing."

"Poor Lou? Poor you. That was about to be something, I could feel it."

"We do have an hour."

"We both know that Lou will be back in 20 minutes. She's sick. There's no shot she stays in there any longer than the courtesy time to finish up and get dressed."

"Aw, I love that you know that."

"Lou is kind of my girlfriend, too. I know enough about her."

"All right, well she better be you're only other girlfriend."

"The only one that counts." He shot her a wink and a smile. "If she's sick, it's probably better if I go. You want to come with?"

"Eh, I think I'll hang back here and she if she needs anything. I'll walk you to the elevator, though."

Once they were both decent, Cecelia now in her pajamas, they left her room and walked hand in hand down the hallway to the lounge where the elevator banks were located.

"I wish you didn't have to go."

"Me too, Cee."

And then he was kissing her again. It was meant to be a goodbye kiss, she knew that, but it escalated way too quickly for either of them to get ahead of. She was melting into him, and she knew he wasn't leaving, not now.

His hands were roaming, air was getting scarce and, through the fog, Cecelia had an idea.

"Come with me."

She grabbed his hand and led him to the end of the hall, into a stairwell and up just one flight.

Her dorm building was located on a river with gorgeous views, especially in the morning. For some reason, rather than being located in the basement as the laundry room had been in her building last year, this one had a rooftop laundry room, if you will.

The washers and dryers were on the very top floor of the building, it was as if the architect had created a sunroom on the roof and somewhere down the line it was given this other purpose. There were thick, old windows everywhere, from floor to ceiling, on the wall opposite the line of washing machines. And, at the moment, it was empty.

Cecelia flicked on the lights and led Max into the room, taking a moment to peer out over the river and take in the night around them.

"This is where you do your laundry? This is the nicest place I've ever seen on campus, this makes no sense."

"Shh, Max. You're missing the point," she turned to face him, "We're alone."

"Oh, are we? Hadn't even noticed."

And with that he was walking her backwards, until she was pushed up against the washing machine that had been feet behind her just seconds ago.

"Your turn, Cee."

He lifted his arms and pulled his t-shirt over his head, laying it carefully down on the washing machine behind Cecelia. Then he was lifting her up until she was sitting atop the machine, Max standing between her legs. He pulled her pajama pants down, exposing her, and dropped them at his side. And then he was kneeling and Cecelia was wrapping her legs over his shoulders, digging her heels into his back.

And as she looked up, she was met with her own reflection in the floor-length window in front of her. Max's strong back flexing as his head moved between her legs and his hands gripped her thighs. She'd never seen herself like this. She never wanted to forget it. Suddenly, her earlier power move had been very sorely outmatched.

They'd sat together on the floor after that, Max leaning against the dryer and Cecelia leaning against Max. He'd put his head next to hers, chin resting on her shoulder as they'd looked out the window. It was as if he wanted to see things how she was seeing them, just to be a little bit closer.

2018
September

These were the things that stuck out the most to her now, as she continued her walk through the city. It wasn't the memories so much as the feelings that had accompanied them. And, as much as love is beautiful and transformative and unique each and every day, it's also about power. It is power. It's power to be different than you were before, to join together and be better. It's the power to help and to heal and to really hold another person up if the time comes that they need it.

The sex held a power all it's own. She'd been a virgin when she met Max and, not that she'd really been saving it for anything in particular, she was so happy that it had been him in the room with her that night.

The experience had changed her. It had left her feeling so vulnerable, but so loved. And just so, so powerful. It was a feeling that she never could reach again. It was that particular, that complex.

She really wished she wasn't thinking about this in the moments before she saw him again. She should've just taken a cab.

CHAPTER 8

2014
May – November

They made it through the rest of their college years without much of a hiccup. There were fights, but they were always the healthy kind; the types of fights that ended in a better understanding of one another or just really good sex. She'd ended up getting an apartment with three friends her junior year and things got even better between them. They had a place to hide out, to cook meals for one another or cuddle up on the couch to watch a movie. These were seemingly adult aspects of a relationship that they hadn't even realized they'd been missing, but just made things more real between them.

They weren't squeezing in time when roommates were away, they were relaxing, they were enjoying one another at their own pace. There was something to be said for slowing things down and savoring them and, after those two years of lazy love, Cecelia was the one saying them.

Graduation snuck up on them, like a thief in the night ready to take them away from the bubble they'd lived in, pretending to be adults when really that world was just ahead of them. And so they donned caps and gowns, said goodbye to their friends and headed back home to their families. That's when things started to creep in, things that would crack the foundation they'd built before they realized anything was amiss; things that would take it all away before either of them was ready.

The first few years out of college are possibly the scariest and most overwhelming of a person's life. It's the first time in twenty-two years that the goal is vague, or not there at all. After a lifetime of working towards graduations, you're finally the graduate. And the graduate, first and foremost, must mourn the child that began the journey. The graduate, the adult, must say, "Thank you for holding on to your dreams, and all of the hard work you had to put in. Thank you for learning to read, and to write, and for keeping your chin up on your not-so-good days."

And then the child must say, "It's up to you now."

And then the child will add, "Please don't forget me. It would be sad if it were all for nothing."

Like most important things in life, there's no preparing for this period of extreme transition. It was a dull and depressing shock. There's no such thing as instant gratification, not anymore. Cecelia missed exams and writing papers, missed the feeling of impressing professors. Life's tough for a teacher's pet with no teacher.

Also tough: trying to feel like an adult in her childhood bedroom. She wasn't a stuffed animal type girl to begin with, all magazine clippings of Ashton Kutcher had been removed from the walls, she'd invested in some beautiful vintage furniture, and still, she felt like a little girl walking around in her mother's high heels.

There was no way for her to really spread her wings and grow into herself in her parent's house. It took her a few months, but she put together a little plan for the very near future. She'd drawn out a budget, and applied to some jobs in New York City.

In the meanwhile, she was waiting tables at her favorite restaurant in town, a little mom and pop shop called The Purple Rose, and putting away anything she didn't spend on her weekly necessities – food, drinks, manicures. Max was bartending at a local dive and she'd grab Lou and swing by most nights just to watch him in action.

She'd loved seeing him change his persona at each stop up and down the bar. The older women got that sweet smile that she'd seen for the first time when he'd invited her to lunch, the younger girls got a charming aloofness and maybe a free shot every now and again. The men got bro Max, as Cecelia called it. All of a sudden, he was talking about sports and cars, calling people "man." That one was the funniest to her, so unlike the person she knew. Cecelia got smug smiles every time a pretty girl leaned in close, as if to say, "I'm not even trying, they just can't help themselves."

It was so interesting to adjust to this new life with him. They weren't college kids anymore, where any relationship can be written off once that graduation song starts up. They were a real life adult couple. It was exciting to think of them in this new way. The relationship had always been serious and so precious to her, but now there was a bigger picture for both of them and, without a conversation or a moment's hesitation, they'd taken that step.

They'd spent their time at college pursuing goals that they'd set before they'd ever even thought of one another. Now, they'd be thinking of a life together, considering one another in any and all major decisions.

By September she'd landed a job with a salary just high enough for her to get her own apartment. She'd be writing social media posts for a large pharmaceutical company. She'd been at the point where she'd take any job that had the word "write" in the description.

And the world spun a bit more smoothly, and the future went a shade brighter on that first day when she took the bus into the city as a working woman. What a feeling of hope and satisfaction to have a salary, and medical benefits, and all of the things that didn't seem all that interesting until she had earned them for herself, until they were supporting her own choices.

She started apartment hunting almost immediately and Max proved to have an impressive knowledge of real estate and building codes. She didn't think about asking him to move in.

She was going to wait for Lou to save up some money, and they'd get a place together. She had years, hopefully decades of them, to live with Max. He could wait.

It wasn't until she'd settled into her new job and decorated her apartment that she realized something was going on. And then it was months before she could admit to herself what it had to be. The only thing that it could be.

She thought she was an adult. She was a woman with a full-time job; she had her own apartment, and paid her own bills. These checked boxes made her responsible; they were proof of her ambition and her drive, but it was Max who would make her an adult. It was his trials, it was the desperate fear that she'd never felt before, it was the decisions that would come to shape her. It was Max who took the last remnants of childhood, who took the lightness from her heart.

And, if someone had asked her before it all started to go south, before she'd gotten the full view of him, she would've sworn that he wasn't capable of these things.

The wooden door to 42 Central, the bar where Max worked, swung closed behind Cecelia, killing the sunlight and leaving the room in darkness save for a few TVs and the dim glow of the overhead strip bulbs.

There were a handful of people scattered along the bar, as was usual for 3 pm, and Max was wiping down the high top tables with a dirty old rag. Sometimes it really was shocking that he was able to make any money at all in a place like this.

"Hey there, handsome," she smiled as she reached Max, leaning in to pop a quick kiss on his mouth.

"I'm at work, Cee," his tone was sharp as he turned, leaving her to awkwardly peck his cheek.

"What? Is your manager here or something?"

"Tom doesn't give a shit what I do. I just don't need to be making out with my girlfriend in front of customers."

"Okay, I'm sorry, Max. It never seemed to bother you before," she was trying to keep the bite out of her voice.

"I'm not bothered, Cee, just trying to work."

"All right, I get it," Cecelia took a step back and leaned on the table next to the one that Max was wiping down. She narrowed her eyes at his back as he leaned across the table to reach the far corner. Was she missing something? It wasn't his birthday, she knew that, but he was obviously taking issue with her and there had to be a reason. "Were you busy at lunch?"

"It was slow for a Saturday, but I had a bunch of guys come in after intramurals so I did okay," Max finished up with the high tops and headed back behind the bar, Cecelia following slowly behind him and grabbing a stool so she could talk to him.

"That's great! I just wanted to stop by and see what time you think you'll be off. I made a reservation at Matthew's so we won't have to wait," she found herself tempted to grab a handful of bar nuts, just to give herself something to do other than wither under Max's annoyed glare. She decided she'd rather look as awkward as she felt than risk ingesting anything that had touched the bar at 42.

"I actually told Jen I'd cover her shift tonight so we'll have to rain check dinner," he didn't even have the decency to look sorry as he said it. Strike two.

"Seriously? We've been talking about this all week," Cecelia tried to keep the whine out of her voice, but she couldn't help that she was disappointed. They hadn't gone out together in longer than she could remember.

"Cee, we can go to dinner another night. It's a Saturday and I need the money. I couldn't pass this up," Max clearly wasn't interested in having a discussion about it. His decision was made and the second he brought up money Cee was left without a leg to stand on. Lest she dare get into the job search conversation with him, which, at the present moment she absolutely did not.

"I know, I just was looking forward to hanging out with you. I feel like we haven't had time together in weeks."

"I'm sorry, Cee. You know I'd much rather be with you tonight, I promise we can do something tomorrow, just us," he had the words down, but the emotion was missing from them. He couldn't give a shit less and she could tell.

"Deal. I'll let you get back to it now. Text me if you have a minute. Bye, Max," Cecelia didn't even bother waiting for him to walk her over to the door, which he normally did when it was this slow. She wanted out. Now.

"See you later, Juice."

"He was really rude, Lou. My feelings were actually kind of hurt," Cecelia was seated next to Louisiana at their favorite nail salon, Magic Spa, as they both soaked their feet in the warm aloe water below them. Whenever they could, the two would grab Starbucks and head over for mani-pedis to freshen up after a week of typing and commuting chipped away at their respective coats of polish.

"I'm sure he didn't mean anything by it. He was probably just having a long day and decided to take it out on you. Not cool, but understandable. He works at freaking 42 Central, I'd be snapping at people, too. Are you sure this color is okay for my skin tone? I'm having doubts," Lou held up the pale pink polish she'd chosen. It was going to look great on her. It was the type of shade that would wash Cecelia right out, but was sure to pop against Lou's darker skin.

"Not helping, Lou. And, yes, I'm sure," Cecelia reached for her iced latte as the technician began massaging her legs.

"I'm not trying to help. You're fine. You're in the perfect relationship, so stop complaining. My boyfriend moved to Oregon, I have real problems," Louisiana narrowed her eyes at the polish one more time before shrugging and handing it back to Lydia, the woman that Lou always insisted on.

"You were going to break up with him anyway!"

"Yeah and do you know how embarrassing that is. I was gearing up to dump him and, not only does he beat me to it, but he did it because he landed his dream job across the country. He wins a thousand times over and I just plain lose. I've said it before and I'll say it again, fuck Joe Hemsley," she'd lowered her voice to a near-inaudible level for that last part and Cee wasn't sure if she was being polite about using the f word or if she was nervous that word would somehow get back to Joe that Louisiana was admitting defeat.

"I thought we were supposed to refer to him as Hoe Jemsley moving forward? What happened to all your 'laugh at his expense' rules?" Cecelia was trying not to giggle as she felt the loofa begin to tickle her foot. She could never keep it together during this part.

"Oh my God, yes! Ugh, that was such a good idea. I'll never not laugh at that. Hoe Jemsley. Genius."

"If you do say so yourself."

"And I do. Anyway, I'm being a bitch. If you're upset with Max, just tell him. He probably didn't realize how much of a dick he was being," and with that powerful statement, Louisiana promptly lost her grip on her iPhone and shrieked as it slid into the water at her feet.

"You like the wine?" Cecelia raised her eyebrows at Max, licking the remnants of her own sip off of her lips.

"Yeah, it's really good. Nice choice, Juice," he smiled across the table, reaching for his napkin and leaning back comfortably in his chair as he laid it across his lap in anticipation of the clams oreganata appetizer they'd just ordered.

"Why thank you. That's high praise from an industry professional such as yourself."

"I'm not sure that bartending at Central puts me up there with the pros, but I'll take it."

It was her opening and she could feel the words on the tip of her tongue. *Speaking of Central, I really don't like the way you spoke to me yesterday when I stopped by.* Or, *Is it really that fucking bad that you have to treat me like shit?* But what was the point?

So he was in a bad mood for one hour of their three-year relationship. Was one crappy conversation worth ruining the whole night?

She decided that it wasn't. She marked yesterday's conversation as a red flag, as something to reference if he decided to go rogue some other time. For now, she was just going to enjoy this night out with Max.

Their conflicting schedules, with her working all day and him working most nights, made it a rare occasion and she planned on sipping her wine and savoring the pasta dish she'd ordered and making Max smile, because that seemed to be what he really needed most these days.

When Cecelia walked into work the next morning, after a night of good food and even better sex, her worries were gone. She and Max had spent the better part of the night laughing and there really was nothing more reassuring to her than the fact that they enjoyed each other's company so damn much.

She even found herself stifling a laugh as she stepped off the elevator, thinking about the story Max had told her about a girl celebrating her 21st who'd puked directly on her best friend the night before. Lou would've had Cee's head.

She strolled past reception, shooting her usual, "Morning, Haley," at the smiling brunette behind the desk.

"Cecelia, wait! These just came in for you, lucky girl," Haley gestured to a bright bouquet of yellow roses. Her favorite.

Her heart skipped a beat as she reached for them. Thanking Haley, she made her way over to her desk and immediately went for the card sticking out between buds.

Sure enough, it was Max's chicken scratch that greeted her.

For my girl,

Hope these flowers get your week off to a better start than your weekend got off to. I'm an asshole and I'm sorry. And I love you. And I love you. And I love you.

- Max

She clutched the note to her chest, savoring the rush of emotion passing through her. Haley was right; she was one hell of a lucky girl.

She pulled out her phone to type a quick message to Max before jerking her computer mouse a bit, bringing the screen to life, smiling all the while.

When Louisiana had called Cee the week before inviting her to a coworker's birthday drinks, Cecelia had given a half-hearted response. It was the kind of sound that even through the phone is accompanied by a shrug and Cee thought that Lou had understood that as a 'maybe' at best. Despite Lou's current claim, Cecelia had no recollection whatsoever of actually agreeing to this.

That hadn't stopped Lou from texting her approximately one million times explaining that a deal is a deal and there's no way that Cecelia would be bailing on her now.

I don't even know any of these people, you have to come with me! I need to infiltrate the work clique and you're going to be my right hand woman.

Truthfully, Cee didn't have any other plans for that night. She'd been looking forward to changing out of the tights she'd worn to work and releasing her toes from the confines of her booties, but that would just have to wait. Lou was being relentless about this and it would be easier for Cee in the long run if she just showed face for an hour, waited for Lou to inevitably 'infiltrate the work clique' and headed home afterwards.

It was through this reasoning that she found herself leaning against a wooden bar in the East Village, vodka club in hand, listening to Lou strategize which of the girls was most likely to warm to her first.

"I've just never had to plan for this kind of thing before, you know?" Lou took a healthy sip of her own drink, a vodka cranberry with an extra lime. "Normally I'm able to just kind of form my own group, but these work cliques are no joke. This is worse than high school. I'm honestly kind of intimidated by them."

"Lou, you're awesome. They're going to see that and you'll be completely fine. Leader of the pack, I bet."

"Thanks for coming. I know I gave you a hard time, but it just makes me feel a lot better having you here."

"Anything for you, Lou," she shot her friend a smile and drained her drink. "I think I'm going to order another one. You in?"

"Hell yeah, I need to get a little lubricated for this."

"Please never say that ever again. It's creepy and if that's the way you've been talking then I'm not surprised you can't make any friends at work."

"That's just plain mean. Although I have to admit I really haven't been myself since Joe left," a worried look crossed Lou's face. "I know I was playing it cool, but I think I might've actually been in love with him. Just wish I would've realized it before he moved away."

"Shit, Lou. I didn't realize you were still thinking about him like that. Have you talked to him at all?"

"A bit. He called me last week and we've sent a few texts, but nothing serious. He seems really happy out there, though. Like 'I'm going to stay here forever' happy."

"He's been gone for less than a month. Give him some time; he's going to miss his friends. And you. Max was always saying that, no matter how unbothered the two of you would act by one another, he'd never seen Joe act like that with any other girl."

"Really? Max said that? Why would you never tell me that?"

"I know you. I thought it might freak you out, so I kept it to myself."

"Saved it for a time that it would be a straight dagger to my heart, did you?"

"That's not what I meant to do, you wacko! Just seems like you could use it now."

"Ugh, look at me. Twenty minutes early to a party at which I essentially plan to beg people to be friends with me and, furthermore, spending that time mooning over Joe Hemsley. This is most definitely a low point in my life, Cee. I'm sorry you have to see me like this."

"Lou, if these past few months are any indication, things are just downhill from here. We might as well get used to seeing one another flailing around. The real world doesn't seem to play around."

"Things not going any better with Max?"

"Things are fine, I just feel like something's off with him. He's been acting normal for the most part, but things feel different to me now."

"Do you think you're still mad about the Central thing?"

"No, I thought it might be that, but I'm over it. Nothing like that has happened again and, looking back, it wasn't that big of a deal. I think I was more surprised than anything else."

"Then what do you think it is?"

"Couldn't tell you. It's starting to get to me though, but what am I supposed to do? I can't pinpoint anything, it's just a feeling I have."

"You guys have been together long enough that you can go to him with it, though. Don't you think? You guys are solid, he's not going to get weirded out if you try to have a talk with him."

"Yeah, you're right. I just don't want to make it an issue until I'm sure it should be. He's really depressed about not finding a job and I don't want to dump anything else on him without a good reason."

"That's probably smart. It really does start to feel personal when no one wants to hire you. I think that's where my confidence issues began, ya know?"

"Lou, be serious!"

"Okay, okay, I'm sorry. But I was only half kidding. You were one of the lucky ones. When months go by and no one's biting it feels like a failure. And then it just starts to get scary, thinking you'll never have a real job and you're falling behind everyone else. It sucks."

"That's definitely a part of it, I think. But it's not like I'm out there living the dream. I hate my job, Monday's feel like some kind of hellscape every week. I never knew I could dread a place so much and still show up there day in and day out."

"That makes me sad. How much longer until you start looking for something new?"

"I want to give it a year. I don't think it'll grow on me, but I wouldn't mind having a new title to put on my resume before I move on."

"That sounds like a plan. Hey, maybe you can come work with me and we can start our own work clique!"

"Only time will tell, Lou. Only time will tell."

"Shit, they just all walked in. Together! So cliquey of them, those cliquey bitches."

"Lou, relax. You're trying to make friends here, remember?"

"Good point. Let me get my game face on."

Before Cecelia knew it, Louisiana was across the bar, warm smile plastered on her face, already winning over the crowd, Cee was sure.

CHAPTER 9

2014
December

"It still doesn't look right to me. I think it needs to be more to the left...or maybe more to the right? What do you think?" Cecelia was crouched down in the middle of her living room, trying to figure out just why her very first Christmas tree in her very first apartment looked so off kilter.

"It's just a crooked tree, Cee. I told you that when you picked it out," Max couldn't hold back a laugh at the look Cecelia shot him in response. She was clearly not as amused as he was by the misfit tree.

"There's no such thing as a crooked tree," she craned her head to the side, trying to find an angle at which her tree looked properly upright.

"That's just categorically false, but I can't get into that right now. What do you want me to do with this thing? My arms are tired from dragging it all over the apartment. I think I got these stupid needles down my pants somehow," he made a show of shaking his leg, as if he were simply crawling in tree needles.

"Not the only needles you have down your pants," she raised her eyebrows.

"Needle?! Once again, *categorically* false," Max fixed her with a look at that. She knew the deal; it wasn't even worth joking about.

"Aw, it's my favorite needle," she blew him a kiss from across the room.

"Keep going, Chapelle. See who fixes your naturally crooked tree then," Max made a show of letting the tree drop to the side an inch or two before he regained his grip.

"Speaking of naturally crooked trees..."

"How about we drop the word 'crooked' from this conversation all together. I think it's starting to hurt everyone's feelings, and I'm including the tree in that."

"Okay, okay! I'll stop. Can you just pull it towards you a tiny bit...there, perfect!" 'Perfect' was probably too strong a word to use, but it would do. She would never admit it, but Max was right. The tree seemed to be the problem, not the stand.

"Yeah?" He let go of the tree all together now, taking a step back to get a better look at it.

"Yeah, come see," Cecelia waved Max towards her, a wide smile on her face at the sight of the tree standing there on its own.

"You're right, it does look kind of perfect," Max stood beside her, hands on his hips, a proud look on his face.

"I love it," she went up on her toes to plant a kiss on his cheek. "Thank you."

"Welcome," he wrapped his arms around her from behind, pulling her against his chest and squeezing her tight. "I love you."

"Love you too, Max," she turned her head to look up at him. "You okay? You look tired."

"Yeah, just a long day. And then I went to my girlfriend's and got verbally abused, so it's just taking a toll on me," she could feel his smile against her neck as he dipped his head and nuzzled his chin at its base, his 5 o'clock shadow scratching her the whole while.

"Aw, you poor thing. Come here, I'll make you some hot chocolate," she turned in his arms, grabbing his hand and leading him to the kitchen where she began warming the milk. Max perched on a barstool, watching her pour their drinks, a glazed look in his eyes.

If Cee was being honest, Max looked more than tired. There was a gauntness to his face that she hadn't noticed before and it was apparent enough to make him look sick. She made a mental note to pay more attention the next time he took off his shirt or wrapped his arms around her. It made her stomach drop to think of collecting information on him like this, to think of putting her suspicions first rather than asking Max for an explanation, but some things were better approached with a bit of evidence and she had a feeling that this was one of those things.

2018
September

She'd made it all the way to 2 pm before her nerves started getting the best of her. Thankfully, the tough part of her day was over. After the successful pitch, she'd suffered through a two-hour meeting, of which, less than five minutes had anything to do with her.

It was just a lot of talk about readership numbers and which writers were pulling their weight, i.e. bringing in the most traffic to the site. Cecelia knew that her team was doing just fine this quarter, and it was always awkward to sit there and witness other editors try to explain why their numbers were down.

This was the one aspect of her job that she truly hated. It was easy to feel pride in high readership numbers, but when eyes weren't coming to your content it had the power to throw the whole team into a funk. Writers stopped focusing on what they thought were the best topics to cover, but rather on what they thought people would be more likely to read.

The lack of interest from the writer inevitably bled through the work itself and it created for some really bland pieces. Needless to say, it tended to do more harm than good to try to please readers rather than write what was going to come across as genuine, at least in her department.

Luckily, she just got a quick rundown of her own team's numbers and, in turn, provided a few comments on how they'd continue to produce similar content while introducing the new series before the editor in chief moved on to the next department. She spent the rest of the meeting imagining the worst possible outcomes of tonight.

She went through dozens of scenarios, from Max completely ignoring her to him pulling her aside to tell her how she'd ruined his life. Neither seemed likely, but anything could happen on a night like this. All it took was the proper mixture of alcohol and emotions.

As the meeting came to a close, Cecelia realized that the worst possible thing that could've happened tonight would be for Max to not be there. That had always been the scariest thought to run through her mind and it remained so to this day. If Max walked into the bar tonight, then there would be no 'worst' outcome happening. And there wasn't much she could do if he hated her now. She wouldn't even blame him. She probably would've felt bitter if he'd left her the way that she'd done him.

She pulled her jacket more tightly around her as a cool breeze passed by, lifting her hair and gently placing it back down around her shoulders. She gave it a shake, encouraging the strands to fall back into their proper place. At least she looked put together, even if her insides were a mess.

She always found that looking good could make up a lot of ground when it came to situations like this. With her makeup done just so and her hair falling in waves down her back, it might not matter that her palms were sweating and her heart was racing. No one would know that she'd been too nervous to eat anything all day. No one would know that she was surviving on one large cup of black coffee alone.

She could stand there in her designer heels and vintage dress with a smile on her face. She could mention her successful pitch and her office with a door and her friendly assistant and no one would have to know about anything else. She might even be able to fool Lou, if only for a few hours.

She didn't need to be the girl who carried a poorly mended broken heart into the bar. She could be the successful editor who just presented an idea to a room of six men and got it through. It was her choice and she knew it.

2014
December

"I'm on my way, Mom. I promise. I just can't get in touch with Max and he was supposed to be here already."

Somehow, Cecelia found herself sitting alone on the couch in her apartment on Christmas morning, picking at her tights and battling an anger that was fast approaching rage. An hour worth of unanswered phone calls and text messages could do that to a person.

"Well, did he know that we were leaving for grandma's at noon?" She could tell her mother was trying to calm her.

She'd ask questions and make suggestions, showing Cee a way to work through it rather than to just be mad about it. Normally, this would just frustrate Cecelia further, but in the moment she was grateful for the pragmatism. Calling a phone that hadn't been answered in more than hour was getting her nowhere.

"Yes, mom. Of course he knows, I've been telling him every day for a month. He was supposed to pick me up an hour ago."

"Do you want to stop by his house? Maybe something happened?" Her mom was still trying.

Obviously, these thoughts had already passed through Cecelia's mind, but she didn't want to start snapping at her mom. It was Christmas morning and she was just trying to be helpful.

Max knew this year was important. It had only been three weeks since her grandfather had passed after a long-fought battle with cancer and she really needed him today. Her grandpa had been the heart of their family and his passing still didn't seem real to her, it just wasn't something her mind seemed to be accepting. She felt like she'd walk into her grandma's house today and see him in the kitchen, fixing himself a drink and making sure no dish went un-taste tested.

But she knew that his absence today would make it more real than it had ever been before. Christmas without him would be unbearable, and she was counting on Max's hand in hers to get her through the day. She knew this and she'd tried to justify Max's lateness with it.

Normally, they'd split their time half and half on holidays. They'd do a few hours celebrating with each family and it always made for a really nice day for the both of them. This would be the first time they'd be heading to just one location, and Max had said that his mom totally understood, but maybe he'd wanted to squeeze in just a little more time. She could understand that. But as fifteen minutes turned into a half hour and now into the hour range, the justification was wearing thin.

"Let me call his mom," It was a last resort and she'd been avoiding it, but she didn't seem to have much of a choice now. "Either way, I'll be over by 12."

"Okay, sweetie. Drive safe, I'll see you soon!"

Cecelia hadn't wanted to call Elaine Maylor. Not for this reason. She really liked Max's mom and was comfortable reaching out to her, but it almost felt like snitching. She could just hear Max now, annoyed and accusatory, making her feel like a child for bypassing him in this way.

But, it was him who had brought her to this and there really was a part of her that was worried about him. He'd hadn't been acting like himself lately, but blowing her off on Christmas was next level douchebaggery and she'd like to think that there had to be a good reason for it. She cursed Max as the phone rang. Max's mom picked up after three rings.

"Good morning, Cecelia. Merry Christmas, honey!" Mrs. Maylor's voice had a warmth to it that always made Cee grateful that this was the woman that Max got to call home to. He always claimed to have an uneventful childhood, and she supposed Elaine was due credit for that.

"Merry Christmas, Mrs. Maylor! I'm sorry to bother you, but I'm having a hard time getting in touch with Max and I was wondering if you could put him on the phone?" She did her best to keep her voice cheerful, she didn't want Max's mom picking up on her annoyance.

"Oh, Max left here about forty minutes ago. He said he was on his way to your place, we sent a few gifts with him in case he forgets and leaves them in the car. Maybe he stopped at the store?"

"Okay, thanks. I'm sure you're right," she wasn't about to tell her that she'd called him nearly twenty times, and had texted him a fair deal greater than that.

"Would you mind shooting me a text if he doesn't get there soon? I'm surprised he isn't answering his phone," Cecelia winced at the hint of worry in Mrs. Maylor's voice.

"Yes, of course. I'm sorry for bothering you!"

"No bother, just please let me know when you get in touch with him. I'll try him too, but he's more likely to answer for you than his mother," she laughed, but Cecelia could hear a distinct lack of humor in it. She was going to kill Max for doing this on Christmas morning.

"Will do! Merry Christmas again."

"Merry Christmas, Cecelia."

Cecelia clicked off of the call and let out a groan. She was already so tired of this day and it was only 11:40 in the morning. She tried Max ten more times, which seemed excessive on top of the past hour's efforts, but she was hoping to avoid the part of this day where she had to cancel her own plans to find him. He didn't answer.

She was about to call her mom and tell her that they'd just have to meet everyone at her grandma's, she couldn't very well just leave without him when he could be lying in a ditch somewhere. She would just have to make the two-hour drive herself once she was able to track down Max.

Her phone buzzed as she opened her recent calls to scan

for her mom's number. It was Max.

I hate to do this, but I feel like shit. I think I'm going to have to miss today and get some rest. Call me when you're back so I can give you your gift. Love you, Merry Christmas

She didn't even text him back. Screw that.

She shot Mrs. Maylor a quick text just letting her know that she'd gotten in touch with Max, and fought back tears as she carried her parents' presents to the car. She bit into her lip as the battle was lost, feeling the December air chill her tears as they rolled down her cheeks.

When she walked into her parents' house, the smile fell from her mother's face.

"Max isn't coming. I don't want to talk about it, I just want to go."

"Okay, honey," and her mom wrapped her in a tight hug, bringing forth another set of tears. It was easier to stop them here though, with her dad in the kitchen whistling a tune over hazelnut coffee and her sister bouncing towards her in what appeared to be an entirely new outfit.

"Cecelia Scott, turn that frown upside down! I look like a million dollars and in just a few hours time we'll be elbows deep in grandma's sour cream cake."

Sedona wrapped her in a tight hug as well, whispering a low, "Screw him, Cee. We'll do an old school Christmas, just me and you," in Cecelia's ear.

She squeezed her little sister back, thankful to call this house, filled with these people, home.

Cecelia spent the day catching up with family, eating the same Christmas meal she'd had since she was child, and laughing with Sedona. Although everyone had been feeling her grandfather's loss and plenty of tears were shed throughout the day, it turned out to be a really great Christmas complete with a light coating of snow falling as they drove home listening to Christmas songs on the radio and singing along in loud, awful voices. By the time she'd said goodbye to her family and headed home to her apartment, she was almost thankful that Max hadn't been there. It was nice to feel like a kid again for a few hours.

She should've just stayed over at her parent's house. Maybe then she wouldn't have reverted immediately back to Max's forgotten girlfriend the moment that she stepped into her apartment. All of the laughter died and she felt wounded in a way that she hadn't allowed herself to process that morning.

Max didn't call her that night, his promise forgotten somewhere throughout the day. Instead, Cecelia curled up in her bed and finally allowed the tears to flow freely. She turned her phone on 'Do Not Disturb' and hoped that at some point over the next few hours Max would find himself frantically leaving voicemail after voicemail on her phone for a change.

It wasn't until the next night that Cecelia saw Max. He showed up at her apartment, looking tired, gift in hand.

"I'm so sorry," when she met his eyes she saw a quiet panic in them. "I don't even know what to say."

"There's nothing you can say. I can't believe you did that to me. I waited here for an hour like an idiot, so excited to give you your gift and now I don't even want to see you," she didn't open the door wide enough for him to enter, gave him no indication that he was welcome.

"Please, just give me a chance to explain. I think I got some kind of 24-hour bug, I can't even remember yesterday. I didn't leave my bed," she was happy to hear the stress in his voice. She'd spent the better part of the day worried that he'd shrug it off, assuming that he'd be forgiven. He understood the severity of what he'd done and it was thawing her.

"Well, that's not true because I spoke to your mom and she said you left your house at 11 to come over here," she met his stress with anger.

"I left at 11 to get cold medicine and it took me a half hour to find a convenience store that was open and then I waited for twenty minutes in line just trying to pay for it," he was rubbing his hand over his face and through his hair, but his voice had taken on a calm.

Her anger had given him an opening. It was something

he'd seen before and knew how to handle. Maybe she should've gone with sadness, he always had a more difficult time working his way through that.

"And you couldn't answer your phone just once during your whole expedition? Couldn't just send me a text so I didn't think something happened to you? I called your mom, Max. I just don't get it."

"I didn't realize you were calling me. I had my phone on silent and it was in the passenger seat. When I got back in the car and saw that you were freaking out, I sent you that text," he was trying to reason with her and it was ridiculous.

She'd realized at some point during the day, when she was overthinking everything and trying to picture the conversation that she was having now, that nothing he could say would make this okay. There was no excuse or explanation that would make sense or justify making her feel the way she'd felt yesterday morning. So her plan was to see if he seemed genuine. If he really appeared to be sorry, then she would move past it. The words 'freaking out' turned that on its head.

"Freaking out? Seriously?" she moved to close the door on him. "I think you should go."

"Cee, I'm sorry, just wait!" His voice was on the rise. "I didn't mean to say that. I'm just trying to tell you what happened."

"And I'm telling you it sounds like bullshit, but I'm not going to fight with you about it. If you say you were buying cold medicine for an hour then I believe you. Why would you lie about something like that," she shot him a look now. "I just don't want you here right now."

"Cee, please. I know that what I did was insane. It was messed up and it's not fair to you, but I missed you. I haven't been able to get out of bed for two days and I just want to be with you. I have your gift and you're going to love it, I know you will. Can I please just come in?"

"I'm just so mad at you," she leaned against the doorframe, letting her arms drop from where they had been crossed against her chest.

"I know. You should be, but do you think we can try to move past this?" he gave her a small smile. "For the rest of our lives, I'll be the idiot who ruined Christmas. Isn't that bad enough?"

"You got that right. This is not a forgive and forget type situation. If I forgive you now, I reserve the right to bring this up forever, in every argument for the rest of time."

"Deal," he took a step closer to her now, making it so that she had to crane her neck to meet his eyes. "Can I please come in now? Pretty please?"

"Okay, come in. As much as I was hating you, I missed you yesterday."

"I missed you, too. I'm so sorry."

"You can't help that you got sick. You just need to stay on top of your phone, that was the biggest thing."

"Got it. No more silencing the ring tone. Now, will you open your gift?"

"I'd be happy to," and she reached out her hands then, letting her first smile of the day spread across her face.

Max had managed to get her a gorgeous gift. It was a small diamond pendant, the kind she could wear every day no matter the occasion or outfit.

"Oh, Max! I love it," she lunged into his arms and squeezed him, reveling in the warmth that she'd missed yesterday night.

"Turn it over," his smile was excited and it sent a surge of happiness through Cecelia.

There, on the back of her beautiful new pendant, was a capital 'M' inscribed into the gold. It even looked like Max's handwriting.

"Wait, did you write that yourself? How did you do this?"

It was so thoughtful and she'd spent the past two days feeling so distant from him that she felt tears coming to her eyes at the sight of it.

"I didn't inscribe it myself, but I gave the jeweler a sample of my handwriting. I wanted you to have something different, so it wasn't just another piece of jewelry."

"It's perfect. I love it. Can you put it on me?" She quickly unhooked the clasp and handed the necklace to Max. She couldn't wait to have it hanging from her neck, his crooked little 'M'.

She gripped the pendant tightly in her hand and leaned in to kiss Max.

"Your turn!" she reached for the fancy envelope she'd been waiting to hand him.

"What could it be, my girl Cee?" He shot her a wink at the rhyme, to which Cecelia jokingly rolled her eyes.

"You'll have to open it up to find out."

Max ripped the envelope with gusto, his eyes lighting up when he pulled out two lower level tickets to Friday night's Knicks game.

"No way! Juice, thank you," He wrapped her up in his arms. "This is awesome!"

"I know you've been wanting to go," she couldn't hold back a proud smile.

"I have been. You're coming with me, right?"

"If you want me to, you can bring one of the guys if you'd rather do that. Totally up to you."

"You're coming with me, Cee."

The tension from their earlier argument erased, Cecelia warmed up two mugs of hot chocolate and spread out a small plate of Christmas cookies for the two of them to share.

It was difficult to lose faith in someone when they'd given you nothing but reasons to trust them for so long. It was so easy to feel the way you wanted to, even when your head is telling you to keep an eye out, something just doesn't seem right.

Cecelia had ample time off between Christmas and New Year's Day, most of which she spent on the couch reading or watching TV. It was so nice to just hang in her pajamas all day, shower, and crawl right into bed with a fresh set of PJs and not a care in the world. It had been so long since she'd had more than a long weekend to relax and, though she could feel herself going stir crazy at times, it was glorious.

Lou had to be in the office for most of Cee's break, but she often stopped by for a glass of wine and to catch an episode of whatever Cecelia was binge watching that day. She inevitably had already seen the episode, no matter which season of which show Cee was on.

It was at 9:30 pm on Tuesday, December 30 when Max let himself into Cecelia's apartment to find Cee and Lou, two bottles of wine deep, giggling. Cee couldn't remember if they were laughing at the TV or one another, but she was pretty sure it didn't matter. Cee looked hopefully at the bag in Max's hand, praying there was enough food in there for she and Lou to share. They were in dire need of some sustenance.

"You guys know that college ended last year, right?" Cecelia let out a scoff at that as Max headed to the kitchen with his mystery bag.

"And what exactly is that supposed to mean, Mr. Maylor?" Cee was slurring only slightly, but it was all in the eyes with her anyway. The second any amount of alcohol hit her system, her eyes started to drift.

"Snuggled up on the couch, drunk on a week night? Just feels like I've seen this scene before," Max's voice traveled from the kitchen into the living room. The sound of plates hitting the counter and the paper bag unrolling was music to Cee's ears.

"You know what, Max? I think I've seen that shirt you're wearing before too. One too many times, if you know what I mean, but I wasn't going to bring it up."

If there was one thing Lou could be counted on to bring to the table, it was a comeback.

Cee clapped her hands in glee, letting out a high-pitched laugh at Max's expense. If Lou had a biggest fan, it was undoubtedly Cecelia Scott.

"It's called an oldie, but a goodie, Lou. Look it up," Max carried the plate of food out to them now, two glorious hamburgers and an entire plate of fries and onion rings.

"Max?" Cee's mouth was hanging open in disbelief. "For us?

Really?"

"I got you covered," he turned back to the kitchen for two glasses of water, placing one in front of each of them, and shot Cecelia a look. She took a sip from her glass, feeling better already.

"Max, I know that I've never told you this before and I really hadn't planned on it if I'm being totally honest, but I do love you. I always have," Lou was speaking over a mouthful of fries, sincerity shining in her eyes.

"Thanks, Lou. Love you, too," Cee could see how amused Max was by all of this and she hoped he could enjoy this night with them too now that he was here. She watched as he bit into his own burger, piled high with more condiments and toppings than she ever bothered to keep track of when he ordered out. For whatever else it lacked, Central really did put out a good hamburger.

This night had taken her back to the million times that she and Lou had split a bottle in their dorm room or their apartment and got that giddy kind of drunk that makes everything funny. She never laughed like that anymore, and it was rare that Max cracked a genuine smile, let alone laughed out loud at something. She wished that Joe were here, or that she'd thought to pick up some of the crappy beer that Max always seemed to drink in college. Anything to bring him back even if it was just for an hour or two.

Cecelia thought that if she tried hard enough, she could convince them all that they were back at school, just for tonight. They could pretend that they were avoiding assignments and that, if they wanted, they could all just skip class tomorrow and not move from the spots they were in now.

2015
January

When the New Year had finally come and gone, Cee found herself at 7 am, struggling to pull it together for work. She was dressed, her hair pulled back in a tight pony tail because there was absolutely no way that she was going to be able to put up a fight against it this morning. She was considering just forgoing the whole makeup ordeal as well, but when one look at the dark bags under her eyes was enough to change her mind.

Max seemed to be drifting in and out of sleep in the bed behind her, tossing and turning. Cecelia finished up with a light layer of makeup and gave herself a once over in the full-length mirror she had hanging on the back of her bedroom door.

In the dim lamplight she looked passable. She gave her ponytail a tug and straightened out her sweater before giving herself a nod. This was as good as it was going to get today.

"I love when you do that," Max's voice was deep with sleep. Cee whipped her head backwards to find him propped up on his elbow, a hand rubbing at his bare chest and a small smile on his face.

"Do what?"

"Whenever you get ready to go somewhere you look at yourself in the mirror like you don't know, like you're not sure if you look okay. But, eventually, you give yourself a little nod and get going. I like the nod. I like when you realize that you look good. Because you always do," he was still smiling at her, but she could see his eyes growing tired again. Seven am wasn't a time that Max Maylor often saw.

"I don't even know if you're awake right now or if that was all sleep talk, but I really needed it," Cee walked over and kissed Max on the lips, morning breath be damned.

"Love you, Cee. Have fun at work," he was definitely crossing the border into sleep talk now.

"Oh I will, Max," Cee laughed. "Love you, too. See you tonight."

2018
September

Cecelia thought of that morning often. Over the years it

had come to serve as the marker in her mind for the last time she could look at Max without reservation. It was the last moment that she had been sure they'd get through whatever was happening between them. She'd left for work that morning feeling full, feeling content.

For a long time, she'd feel this deep envy for the girl that had walked casually to the bus that morning; so secure in the small world she'd built for herself. She was jealous of the happiness, which felt as though it had been hard fought at the time, but she had no clue what it was to fight for anything back then. Her battles had been nothing when compared with all that she'd faced since then.

Even now, she wasn't sure she'd ever be that content again. It was the kind of bliss that only ignorance could bring. The days and months that followed had shaken her, had exposed her to a side of herself that she would've rather never met. There was no forgetting it. There exists a sadness, strong like death. She knew this now. The fear of its return is all consuming. Each step forward comes with the fear that it will take you back.

She could feel that fear rising in her now. She was too close, just a few blocks away from the restaurant, just a few minutes away from Max. Her hands were starting to grow warm from their place in the deep pockets of her jacket.

She didn't know what would be worse, if they spoke or if they didn't. She couldn't risk being close to him again, but it was what she wanted more desperately than she'd cared to admit these past few weeks. She missed Max with the same intensity that had always accompanied her thoughts of him.

More than the fear, there was hope in her tonight. Hope that maybe she'd made the right decision back then, that creating space between them to become the people they were supposed to be was necessary, and maybe their time was now.

CHAPTER 10

**2015
March**

There are only so many times that a person can apologize for the same thing. Max had sent flowers to her four months ago after he'd snapped at her in the bar. He'd hit it out of the ballpark on his very first swing and now he had nothing left to give. Because you can't buy flowers every time you mess up if it happens every day.

They meant something to her that first time. But now he was jumping down her throat at an almost constant rate. It was over everything, it was mostly over nothing. The TV was too loud, she was moving around too much when they were watching a movie together on the couch, she was taking too damn long to get ready before dinner.

"Seriously, Max?" she shrieked through the bathroom door. "You know I have to leave for work in five minutes. Come on!"

Maybe she was being overdramatic, maybe she was being too loud for 7am, but the look on his face when he swung the door open wasn't warranted. She couldn't really think of anything that she was capable of doing that would warrant that look.

It was murderous, full of this insane rage that she hadn't ever seen in him before.

"Are you fucking kidding me right now? You're going to scream like a 2-year-old and stomp your feet. Grow up and quit being such a bitch, Cecelia. You're embarrassing yourself and annoying the shit out of me."

"What?" she was dumbfounded. There was no other word for it.

"You heard me. You're acting like a moron."

And she couldn't help it, she burst into tears right there, storming past him and slamming the bathroom door shut behind her. She braced her arms against the sink and took a deep breath as she looked into the mirror facing her. Her face was already tear-stained, the light layer of makeup she'd applied wearing away before she'd even stepped foot outside of her apartment.

There was a slow drip coming from the faucet below her and a light buzz coming from the toilet, which did always seem to take a good five minutes to fully flush. The small window in the wall opposite Cecelia was cracked open and she could hear cars and voices carrying themselves up from the street below. There was blood pounding in her ears from the rapid pumping of her heart against her chest. There was no apology. There was no breathing, no words, coming from the other side of the door. He'd simply walked away.

She'd left for work that morning without saying a single word to him. She wiped her eyes, touched up her makeup and walked out the door.

Her day had been predictably awful, her stomach in knots over the call that hadn't come, the *I'm sorry* text that never sent her phone buzzing. Did he not realize how bad that had been? She almost had herself convinced that it hadn't happened at all. Maybe she'd sat on the couch to put her shoes on and nodded off for a split second. Maybe the whole thing was just a bad dream.

She always had these weird, vivid nightmares whenever she couldn't get herself up with her alarm. For every morning that she allowed herself just that extra fifteen minutes back in dreamland, it was a nightmare that met her instead. And it was always a nightmare just like the one that had taken place this morning; so real, but with a few tips of the hat. There were just one too many things that didn't quite add up. That's what it felt like and, no matter how long she avoided small talk and emails dinging in on her desktop, she couldn't actually believe that he'd spoken to her that way.

He'd called her a bitch and he'd meant it. He'd called her a moron in just the same way. She could almost laugh at how ridiculous this all was. At how thirty seconds could make her question three years.

Her palms were sweating when she walked into her apartment that night. She couldn't be sure that Max was still there, but something told her that he hadn't left. She knew he didn't have any shifts at the bar and it had become normal for him to sit around that apartment on days like this, watching TV or, more frequently, not leaving bed at all.

Sure enough, she could see through the crack in her bedroom door that he was still in there, watching a video on his phone. The nerve it took for him to be casually snuggled up in her bed after the way their morning had gone made her want to grab for a frying pan on her way into the room. Maybe a good whack upside the head would do him some good.

As she approached the room, Max's shoulders tensed with awareness, but he didn't look up. His face remained passive, his eyes glued to the phone.

"You've been in bed all day?"

She didn't bother to hide her disgust. It was coming out of her in every which way, and she was glad for it. He wasn't worth the effort it would take for her to be civil right now.

"Nothing gets past you, Cee," her name on his lips had her cringing.

"Max, look at me," and he did, with the same dazed look that he'd been wearing around for weeks now, maybe months.

"What the hell is going on with you? You tore me apart this morning and you didn't think that I deserved an apology?"

She wanted to cry again. She couldn't, she knew that, but

the tears were putting up a good fight.

"I'm sorry, Cecelia," he all but grumbled it, as a 5-year-old would after being reprimanded for throwing sand or pulling her.

"Not good enough. Not by half," the tears were turning angry, her voice taking on a different tone.

"You don't get to talk to me like that, ever. No matter what's going on, you don't get to do it. Obviously something's the matter with you and I'm sorry, I really am, that you haven't been able to talk to me about it, but that falls on you. I'm here. I love you and I always want to help you, no matter what you're going through. But you can't keep it to yourself and then take it out on me. I didn't sign up for it and I won't stick around for it," she hadn't planned on taking it that far, but she found herself meaning every word.

"Nothing's going on with me, Cecelia. We got into an argument, it happens."

"That wasn't an argument, Max! This is an argument. Where two people take different sides and hash it out. What happened this morning was... I don't know. I can't even explain it. An outburst? An attack? You looked at me and called me a bitch after I asked you to let me in the bathroom."

"Asked me? You were pounding on the door!"

"Oh please! That's how I am in the morning. I'm hyper. I'm always running late."

"So you can yell, but I can't?"

"It wasn't the same. Maybe if I'd said 'Max, you stupid bastard, let me in the bathroom' it would've been a different story. But it wasn't the same and you know that."

"I don't know what you want me to say here. I apologized. I'm sorry, I shouldn't have said it, I take it back."

"Can you, for one second, act like you understand that this is serious to me?"

"I'm right here. I can see that you're taking this very seriously."

"No, you're *not* right here, Max. You haven't been right

here in a long time. Fix this or get the hell out of my apartment and don't come back until you figure out what the hell you want."

And, as Cecelia walked to the kitchen and popped the cork on a bottle of red, Max threw on his hoodie, laced up his sneakers, and walked straight out the door.

Three absolutely miserable days went by before she heard from him again. It felt like three years. It felt like hell.

Cecelia went to work, went home, and went to bed. She knew she'd be much better off making plans and staying busy, but she didn't seem to have the energy or the focus to so much as maintain a normal conversation. What little she could do, she saved for the hours that she spent in the office.

Her work, if not perfect, was at least acceptable and she was fine with that. She was a good employee. She completed her assignments quickly and accurately; she went the extra mile whenever she could squeeze it into her schedule. So, if her personal life got in the way for a few days, well that was just the cost of hiring humans instead of robots to work for you.

She, of course, told Louisiana that she'd had it out with Max, but she kept it to herself otherwise. As someone who'd been on the receiving end of quite a few complaints about friends' boyfriends, she knew that an image was tainted very easily. It could become a slippery slope to go to friends with each and every falling out. Before you knew it, you'd have very few people rooting for your relationship.

And she wanted people rooting for her and Max. She was rooting for them. But this was completely new territory. The arguing, the not speaking, none of it was familiar to her. She didn't know how to handle it. But she did know that she wasn't going to be the one apologizing. She was giving him the time it took to come to her. It was tough, especially when all she wanted to do was call him every second, but this was an important moment in their relationship.

This was a chance to keep the scales even, to demand the respect that she wanted to have. She couldn't be the one to apologize. This had all begun because she decided to stand up for herself and that was all the reminder she needed to keep her from reaching for the phone.

Cecelia's phone rang at 8:25 pm that third night. She'd just finished washing the dishes she'd used for dinner and was headed for the shower when she heard the sound of the buzzing phone against the granite countertop. She was right in that sweet spot, where enough calls and texts had come in and had turned out to not be from Max, that she wasn't really counting on this one being him either.

But it was his name displaying across the top of his screen, her favorite photo of him beaming at her from behind it. She nearly let it go to voicemail.

She wanted to talk to him, to finally fix whatever had broken between them the other night, but she didn't know what she was going to do if that wasn't what he wanted. He could very easily be calling to tell her that he needed space. With the way he'd been acting, that seemed to be the most likely course of action to take.

He didn't seem too keen on the idea of her helping him with whatever had been bothering him. She didn't think they'd have gotten to this point if he'd been open to that. And if she couldn't help him, or more importantly, if he didn't think that she could help him, then what was the point of their relationship anyway. If they couldn't weather this one storm, their first serious one, then whatever they had between them amounted to nothing.

She answered the phone, of course. She couldn't put herself through this anymore, not when he was reaching out. If he wanted to end it, then better for her to know now so that she could start dealing with it. So that she could pack a bag and go stay at her parents' house and hug her mother and cry herself to sleep in her childhood bed, as she'd been tempted to do each night this week.

"Hello?"

"Cee, hey. Wasn't sure if you'd pick up," his voice was tentative, unfamiliar.

"Me neither."

"I'm glad you did. I just wanted to see if you were home. I think we should talk, in person."

"Yeah, I'm here. I just finished up with dinner," Cecelia did her best to keep her voice even, his request making her feel suddenly very small.

"Okay, great. Is it okay if I come over?"

"Sure, I'm just going to take a quick shower, but I'll be out in 10."

"Okay, see you in a few."

"See you," Cecelia clicked off her phone and gently placed it down, bringing her hand up to rub at her mouth, her heart jumping up to her throat.

Cecelia hurried through her shower, washing her hair and soaping up her body in record time. It probably would've made more sense for her to skip the shower and mentally prepare for what was about to happen, but she needed to feel clean. Her commute home had left that familiar layer of grease and grime on her and she didn't want to have this particular conversation in that state.

So she lathered her hair in her favorite lavender shampoo and used the vanilla body wash she'd picked up from the drug store the day before. She let the warm water run over her skin and rolled her shoulders back, releasing the tension from the day. She leaned her head back and let the water hit her face, holding her breath and forcing her mind to go blank. She didn't think about Max. She didn't worry that she'd have to start over and find someone else to love.

By the time she'd dried off, smoothed a generous layer of lotion over her skin and threw on a pair of cozy sweats, there was a light knock coming from her apartment door. She headed for the hallway, tossing her wet towel in the hamper on the way, and took a deep breath as she opened the door.

"You look about as nervous as I feel," Max joked as he walked through the now open door, pausing to drop a hesitant kiss on her cheek, as if she might turn her face away at the last second.

He didn't pull his head away though. Instead, he dropped it down onto her shoulder, hands still at his sides and breathed in.

"I really missed you, Cecelia," this was new, too. This sadness. It must have come with the anger. Max and all these new emotions, who could keep up.

She still said nothing.

Instead, she closed the door and guided him to the couch, sitting cross-legged with her body turned towards him, but not as close as she normally would have, not tonight.

"First, I just want to tell you that I'm sorry, I'm so, so sorry for the way I spoke to you. For the things I said to you. I was terrible and you didn't deserve it."
He was shaking his head in disbelief, as if he couldn't quite stomach the fact that he'd treated her that way.

"I've been taking a lot of things out on you and I'm not going to do it anymore. I can't do it anymore," she could hear his voice getting thick and she really hoped he didn't start crying here and now. She needed to get through this with what little strength she had left. If he cried, it would all go out the window.

Cecelia had seen Max cry exactly twice in the past three years. Once, when he'd realized he just wasn't going to be able to pull his calc grade to the point of passing, and the other time when his mom called to tell him that his grandfather had passed away. Both times he'd waited until the two of them were alone. Both times Cecelia had held him close to her and rubbed his back until he calmed down. She was prepared to do the same for him now, but that would take everything in a different direction.

"I just want to help you, Max," she reached for his hands, wrapping both of her hands around his so they were clasped together in his lap.

"And I want to let you, but I don't know how to. Not with this. I don't even think I can get the words out."

"It's okay, Max. You can tell me anything. It's going to be fine, I promise."

He seemed to steel himself against what was about to happen, pulling his hands from hers and turning to face her fully. And then he spoke and it truly did change the rest of her life.

2018
September

When Cecelia had finally gathered the nerve to log off of her work computer and sign out for the day, it was at the very last moment. She'd spent the afternoon completing small tasks and getting herself in a good position to start next week off. It was a typical afternoon and she wished she'd had more work piled up to distract her, but she simply didn't.

She stared at the blank screen for a moment before heading out to tell Kevin that she was done for the day if he wanted to go. He nodded his thanks, grabbed his coat and told her to have a nice weekend. She'd have to talk to him about leaving earlier, rather than waiting until she headed out, especially as the week was coming to a close.

Cecelia then wandered down the hall to Stan's office, just to be sure that he didn't need anything from her before they headed into the weekend, but the room was empty, his work bag nowhere in sight. Good. Hopefully he was taking Greg out to a nice dinner.

She re-entered her office and hesitated before grabbing her dress off of its hook and heading for the restroom. It wasn't until that moment, when the rest of the day was behind her, leaving nothing between her and the party, that she forgot herself. Cecelia felt the weight of all the darkness she'd overcome in that walk through her office building's halls.

Cecelia Scott had known Max Maylor like she knew the moves to every routine performed in the movie Bring it On. It was nearly down to a science, it was without fault. She'd known his thoughts, his mannerisms, the way his body moved when he wasn't paying attention, and the way it moved when he was. She couldn't quite figure out if she'd been willfully blind to the one thing that mattered, or if, the more likely scenario, she just had no way of identifying the symptoms.

It was funny, or ironic might be a better word for what exactly it was, but she would never have guessed this. Of all of the worst-case scenarios that had run through her mind, not even in her wildest dreams would this have happened.

Those words delivered that night, days and months and years ago now, were enough to have her shaking her head in disbelief. And then, as it always did, the disbelief gave way to fear. And, not for the first time since Lou had told her about the party, she considered that Max might not be all right when she saw him again.

And just the thought of that possibility had the haphazard strands of thread and strips of tape holding her heart together loosening even further.

2015
March

"No, Max. This doesn't make any sense," she found herself backing away from him, standing up to gain any leverage at all in this moment.

"I don't know how else to say it. I've thought it about it for three days and then I just missed you and it wasn't going to come out the right way anyway so I just had to tell you, straight out," the tears were there now, making their way down his face, but she couldn't take the necessary steps in his direction. She couldn't go near him.

"I understand if this is too much. If you need time or space I can give you that. Whatever you want," his eyes were set on her, pleading. "Whatever you want."

"I just need a second. Just give me a minute to think."

"I can go. Do you want me to go?"

"How long, Max?" she felt the words come out rather than

heard them.

"A while. Years. But recently it's worse than it's ever been," He seemed to be better prepared for this part of the conversation. Or maybe it was just the fact the she hadn't asked him to leave.

"Do your parents know?"

"Yes."

"What is it? What are you taking?"

"Painkillers. Oxycontin," and his head dropped to his hands. "God, I'm so sorry, Cee. I'm so sorry."

"I don't understand. How did I not know? I'm with you all the time. I know you. How did I not see this?"

And that's when she felt it for the first time; the fear.

It was unfamiliar, overwhelming in its emergence, but it would become a part of her. She would carry it with her from the moment she woke up to the moment she climbed into bed at night.

It would bring nightmares to her and keep her awake. It would turn away food and sap her energy. It would take a bit of her faith and replace it with a bone deep sadness, with the realization that all it would take is the slightest turn for her world to fall completely on its side.

"There was no way, Cee. Please don't do this to yourself. I've been hiding it for so long, it's like second nature to me. But, it's gotten so far out of my hands and I don't know what to do. I have a problem and I think I need help now."

"Just tell me what to do and I'll do it. Max, just tell me what to do," but she was sobbing now and he was walking towards her. He wrapped her in his arms and rested his tear-soaked face on top of her head and they just stood there until they were too exhausted to stand.

And then she led him to her bed because he was right there in front of her and there was an edge to her gratitude for that in this moment. She never wanted to take her hands away from him again. She wanted to look at him forever and make sure he wasn't going anywhere, not without her.

This was before she could truly understand the severity of the situation. This was before she'd associate the word relapse with Max. This was *before.*

Max was a freshman in college, 18 years old, the first time he ever took a pill. It was a mistake, he'd told her. It was the worst mistake he'd ever made in his whole entire life. But it was also common.

As stunned as she had been to learn of Max's drug use, it wasn't something that she hadn't heard before. Teen boys with a little bit of money to spare. Bored kids feeling reckless. It happened.

She'd heard about it for years. Hell, it was on the news. They'd held assemblies on addiction in high school and, she was fairly certain, there was a skit done about it at freshman orientation.

But it's one of those things, like plane crashes and earthquakes, that seems to affect other people. It seems impossible that this terrible fate could ever befall you. And then it does. And, nine times out of ten, by the time you realize what you're up against you're in way too deep to simply walk back out.

Max had told her plenty of secrets. The time he'd gotten suspended from school for punching his ex-girlfriend's new boyfriend. The fact that, as much as he missed his parents and his sister when he was away at school, he missed his dog a little bit more. His aversion to heights ever since he fell out of a tree when he was thirteen. But this was a piece of darkness; he thought it might even be a deal breaker. He wasn't just confiding, he was confessing.

She knew he dabbled in drugs when he was in high school, he'd told her as much when they'd first gotten together. He'd never made it sound like anything serious. No mention of rehab or interventions. Just some comments about some weekends that got a little bit too wild, and a lot of wasted pizza delivery money.

She had never even thought to dig deeper into the subject. As far as she knew, he'd been sticking strictly to alcohol since they met freshman year of college and, if he had been high a time or two, it was never the scary kind of high she'd seen some kids get. Where they're completely zombied out, they're tongues like dead weight in their mouths while they tried to string nonsensical words together.

That seemed to be where the missing pieces began to slip away. Because she had a few very clear pictures in her mind of what it was to be high and Max hadn't fit any of them.

His eyes weren't bloodshot; his words were, if anything, sharp. Not the wild, philosophical musings that weed could give way to, not the intense ramblings that she'd associate with cocaine. He was angry, he was zoned out and he was tired. He was selfish and reclusive. He was changing and this had been the cause and she just had no idea.

But, she told herself, it really didn't matter. There was no going back and changing things. There was no work to be done in the past. This was happening and he was asking for help. That was the first step and, when they woke up that next morning, Max sleeping soundly next to her, she was ready to stand by him.

He looked like a child, as most people tend to while asleep. His hair was pushed pack off his face and his breathing was low. She put her hand to his chest and felt his heart beating. He'd been so sick and no one had even known. That was the goal; just keep his heart beating.

In that moment, Cecelia had stepped onto a carousel. And you don't just step off a carousel in motion. You have to brace yourself. You have to gather up your courage, and then you have to jump off mid-spin and pray you meet solid ground.

CHAPTER 11

2015
March

Cecelia was just about ready for work when she heard Max moving around in the bedroom. She'd decided to let him sleep in. It sounded like the past three days had been decidedly worse for him and she knew the exhaustion that could come from worrying. She'd been there many a time and there was nothing better for it than a restful night's sleep, which he seemed to have gotten.

She slid her earring back onto the diamond stud she had pressed to her lobe and walked over to the bedroom, peaking her head in as Max put his feet on the ground and sat up on the edge of the bed.

"Morning," she tried to send him an encouraging smile. One that let him know she loved him no less for what he'd told her the night before. She was finding, as the shock of it all wore off, she loved him more for his honesty, felt even more endeared to him for the fear she'd seen in his eyes.

"You look beautiful," he was still feeling off, she could tell.

"Thank you. I'm heading out. Do you have work today?"

"Yeah, I go in at noon."

"Okay, come over tonight?"

"Definitely," she could tell he was thankful for the invitation and the united front that it implied.

"Good. I love you, Max. So much. I'll see you tonight," with that she crossed the room to land a kiss on his lips. He gripped her hand as she turned to leave and just held on for a beat. Cecelia gave him a smile as she turned to leave the room, feeling hopeful.

He was sick. That was it. He'd come over tonight and they'd talk it through. They'd research rehabs and make a plan. Hell, maybe he already had one. He said his parents were aware of what was going on and she knew Mrs. Maylor. She wasn't the type that would sit idly by and let her son succumb to this. She felt her heart surge a bit at the thought; she wasn't alone in this.

She wasn't the only person in the world who loved Max desperately and needed him, here and healthy. There was someone else in their corner who had even more at stake.

It wasn't until she was seated on the bus, headphones in and head resting against the seat behind her that the tears came. Max was sick.

Cecelia's day did not improve from there. Her boss was stressed about his writers missing their upcoming deadlines and there were already four very timely assignments on her desk by the time she got into the office. She spent the day sourcing images and outlining preliminary formats, using guesswork to picture how long the articles would be based on the writers' estimates.

She set up meetings with each writer, which required the booking of eight conference rooms, which was no easy task in an office that only boasted four rooms that had the screen her boss would need. She sat in on each meeting, taking notes and putting new deadlines and follow-up meetings in her boss, Phoebe's, calendar. If she hadn't been asked to attend the meetings, she would've gotten out on time, but she ended up staying an extra hour catching up on emails and making sure that Phoebe had everything she'd need over the next few days.

She'd texted Max on her way home and learned that he'd be another few hours. So she whipped herself up a salad with a few slices of grilled chicken on top and settled in for her Thursday night shows.

Though she was fine herself, there was something about this whole situation that was making her feel the need to burrow into her blankets and drink a cup of tea and never move again.

She wouldn't be telling anyone about what Max had told her the day before.

There was a part of her that felt like it wasn't her secret to tell. But there was also a part that didn't want anyone to know for her own personal reasons. She didn't want to hear her friends' opinions; she didn't want to have her parents telling her to leave him. This was one of those things that just didn't translate well. She didn't think that anyone, not even Louisiana who was about as understanding as they come, would be able to accept this.

She knew this because, had Louisiana come to her with this same issue, she would tell her she needed to take care of herself. There was a label for Max now that she really didn't want to think about, but she knew everyone else would call this was it was. Max was a drug addict. And she really couldn't think of one person in her life that wouldn't hear that and do everything in their power to pull her away from him.

And it wouldn't matter that he wasn't *like that*. It wouldn't matter that he'd come to her and asked for help. It wouldn't matter that they'd known him for years and been around him while this was going on and hadn't noticed a thing.

It would only matter that he was posing a danger to her, bringing something potentially deadly into her every day life. And so she wouldn't put any of them in that position. She'd shield them from this and, in turn, shield herself (and Max) from them.

By the time Max got to her apartment that night she was half asleep and he looked to be in the same state, but she wanted to have this conversation with him. She needed to know that action was being taken. If he was thinking that they could just go back to normal and she would take a back seat with this, he was sorely mistaken.

She made them both a cup of tea. She knew Max would only take a sip or two. He wasn't really a fan of it and never had been, but it always comforted her to have a steaming mug in her hand when she was feeling scared.

"I know we're both exhausted, but we have to talk. I need to know what's going to happen now."

They were sitting at her dining room table, which was small and round and only had room for two chairs. It reminded her of the type of seat you'd have at a small café and, though it was just shoved into the corner of her kitchen, it made her feel fancy, maybe a bit Parisian, to sit at it with a cup of coffee each morning.

"I'm going to stop. I've been talking to my parents and I'm taking the next week or so off of work to get off of everything. My mom is going to stay with me and I'm going to get better. I promise you. I know I scared you yesterday, but I have this under control. You don't have to worry. I'm just going to be MIA for a few days and probably feeling shitty for a while, but I'm committed to it this time."

Max was gripping his mug with both hands, a serious look in his eye.

"That's it? You don't think you need like professional help?" Cecelia was trying to keep her voice even, optimistic.

"We talked about it, but it's something I'd rather do on my own. Rehab can be a bubble. A lot of people go in, get clean, but then get back home and the bubble pops and they go right back to it. I need to do this my way," Max seemed sure and it was pushing the fear from her stomach. His confidence always had a way of convincing her that things would be fine.

"If that's what you want, then I'm here for you. I'm going to help any way that I can."

"I'm going to do this for you, Cee, and we're going to be good again. I'm going to be good to you again."

"I just want you to be okay. I got really scared today thinking about what could happen if you can't stop."

"I know, I'm scared, too."

"We got this."

"We do. Everything is gonna be fine," and he leaned across the table and kissed her head and she hung onto every word, like an idiot.

Lesson one: you really can't trust an addict to tell the truth, they're masterful liars, if nothing else.

CHAPTER 12

2015
April

There's very little that can be done for someone who won't help himself. She was exhausted by the day before she even got out of bed. But that's to be expected when you spend half the night with your hand hovering gently over your boyfriend's nose just to be sure he's breathing correctly.

Last month, when Max went off the grid for four days and came back to her looking like he'd come down with some kind of soul-sucking disease, she felt that she was in the thick of it. This was recovery, the hardest part, and it would be bad before it got any better. He'd spent the next two weeks feeling and looking like absolute shit. He could barely keep food down and his skin was so pale it looked translucent.

But, then, miraculously, he was feeling better. He looked like his old self again and his mood had improved by leaps and bounds. She'd been so grateful for those few days, before it hit her. His old self was not who Max should be looking like. But she couldn't bring herself to accuse him.

Things were so good and he seemed so happy for the first time in so long. What if she was just being crazy? She'd never been in this situation before. It was very possible that this was just the next step in the process. So she said nothing. She watched him closely though. She kept an eye on his weight, waiting for him to start filling out. She'd read that was important, that was a sign of good health. But that was something that could take weeks and, in the meantime, she became convinced that he was using again.

Cecelia wanted to tell Max that he needed to start sleeping at his own house, that she needed a little bit of space. But she didn't want him to know that she was as worried as she was, and she wasn't sure that she could sleep if there wasn't anyone there to watch Max through the night.

He was looking worse every day. He wasn't stopping, she became sure of it. And who could she talk to that wouldn't take it out of context, who wouldn't allow it to taint the image that Max was trying to keep up to everyone but her.

And so she went back to him and she took a different approach this time. She wouldn't get through this if the conversation went as the last one did, with both of them cut wide open and crying.

"Please be honest with me, I think you're still struggling and, if that's the case, we need to do something. Now."

"Maybe I've slipped up a few times, but I promise things are better than they were. I'm still getting better."

"I'm not playing, Max," shoulders squared, chin up, this was the only way to do it, "You look terrible, you look *sick*. This has to stop. This can't be the way our life is."

"I'm trying, Cee. I'm really trying, but it isn't the easiest thing in the world to do, believe it or not," there was a gentle bite to his words. He didn't necessarily want to deal with this either.

"I know that. I've been doing a ton of research. I'm trying to understand what you're feeling, and I've been reading a lot of articles about how to handle this. I want to help you. If you're still against rehab, then I think we can do this together. But this won't be like the last time." She was doing her best not to patronize him, not to treat him as a sick baby, but that's how she saw him now.

"When did you start taking the pills again?"

"Is this necessary?"

"When?" he rested his head back, defeated, before he responded.

"I never stopped. I tried to just cut back that week that I spent at home, and it was killing me. I needed more. I felt like I was dying without it, Cee, I had to have it for just a little while longer."

"Wait, what? You never stopped? I thought your parents were watching you?"

"They were, but my mom's students had some kind of state testing coming up so she couldn't take too much time off and my dad was working from home, but he was distracted for most of the day. I told him I was getting some fresh air and I just would go around the corner, get what I needed, and come back."

"Christ, Max."

"I was trying, Cee. I was taking less for a few weeks, I just couldn't stick to it and I didn't know how to tell everyone and put you guys through all that shit again."

"Max, this can't happen. You have to really stop now. I'm not kidding. I can't handle this. I haven't even been sleeping."

"That's why I didn't want to tell you. I know you're more affected than you let on and it's not fair to you."

"Are you willing to do this for real now?"

"I don't think I have a choice."

"Wrong answer, but you're right. You don't have a choice. We're going to do this my way now. Do you understand?"

Every inch of his 6 foot 3 inch frame had lost its power. He was so thin, and he looked weaker every day. Especially in this moment. He looked no more than a child as she explained to him that she would be taking the week off from work, as would he. He would not be leaving her apartment and no one was to be buzzed in.

There wasn't much that she could do to ease his pain, but she would be spending the week focused on making him as comfortable as possible as his body went through the torture of withdrawals. He looked even younger when he simply nodded and pulled out his phone to call his boss, to text his coworkers and ensure that his shifts at the bar would be covered.

Cecelia took this time to go into the bathroom and splash some cold water on her warm face. She clenched her hands together to stop them from shaking. She wanted to call her mom and hear her say that she was proud and that Cecelia had been brave. She wanted to call Lou and ask if she was able to handle this. Instead, she unclenched her hands and went to lay them on Max's shaking shoulders. She pressed them to his cheeks to catch his tears before they reached his chin.

"You're okay, Max. Hey, I promise it's going to be all right. You're going to be fine, just let this pass," Cecelia whispered over Max's sweat-soaked head, her whispered breaths sending a wave through his hair.

She clutched his shaking bones to her chest and tried to steady him against the chills that were wreaking havoc on his body. She was expecting this. The chills, the fever, the vomiting, this was all so normal. This was his body fighting against chemical dependency. This was his body fighting. And this was her fighting too, in the only way she could.

Day two post-pills was proving to be worse than the first.

"Cee, I can't do this anymore. I don't think I can take this. I think it's too much. I feel like I'm going to die," she could see the fear in his eyes.

"It's going to be fine, Max. It's going to be so worth it. You just have to get through the hard part and you'll be like a new person. I promise. I promise, Max." And her voice was shaking and she was feeling the anxiety coursing through her body because what if he wasn't okay? Maybe she *should* take him to the hospital, or at least call his mom. But that wasn't part of the deal.

She wanted this to work so badly, and she felt like any interference would jeopardize this opportunity to fix him. It was as if she'd forged this connection with him over the past few days and adding anything else to the mix would break the spell. And, as far as she could tell, this was all normal.

ONE TIME, BADLY

He didn't seem to be feeling anything that wasn't explicitly stated in the research that Cee had done. If it came to that, she would think of next steps. For now, he was on course. He was in the depths of hell, from what she could tell, but the only way out was through.

So she stayed strong. She told her parents and her friends that they'd both gotten the flu. She talked her mom out of dropping off soup and gingerale. She kept the lights low and made as little noise as humanly possible. She logged onto her laptop and tried to keep up with work emails as much as she could and she anxiously cleaned her apartment, over and over again.

She changed the sheets at least twice a day, they were sweat-soaked and stale and it gave her something to do for the long stretches of time that Max was just laying there, dozing or moaning or looking at the wall with that awful expression on his face. As if she'd made him sit through the most boring history lesson in the world, but put hot coals under his feet for the duration.

For his part, Max acted as she'd expected. He spent his time begging for drugs or forgiveness, begging for forgiveness for begging for drugs. He had no interest in anything. He didn't want the TV on, he didn't want any music playing. He wanted the lights off and the blinds closed. But most of all he wanted painkillers.

She'd cleared the cabinets of everything, even things that seemed harmless. They had no Advil, no Tylenol, no Midol, not even a cough drop was left at the bottom of the medicine cabinet. The only pills in the apartment were her birth control pills, but she wasn't willing to part with those and there wasn't anything that he could get from them anyway.

Still, she made sure the case was hidden at all times. No need to bring the thought of prescriptions and all that they entailed to the fore of his mind any more than they already were.

Cecelia whipped her head around as she heard her bedroom door creak open and Max's slow, heavy footsteps make their way to the bathroom. She'd been sitting on the couch reading a book, but she was pretty sure she was on the same page as yesterday. There was no part of her brain that could focus on the words and string them together.

She quietly made her way down the hallway, stopping outside the bathroom door and listening for any signs of a problem. He didn't seem to be gagging so that was good, but she couldn't hear anything at all which was possibly not good. She would've heard him if he'd fallen over though. Or at least she thought so.

No, no, she shook her head. There would've been at least a small thud if Max had passed out and that was being generous. The man was well over 6-feet tall, the thud would've been much more than small.

She gave it a few minutes before she called out to him. There was no response, so she stepped forward and knocked lightly on the door.

"Max?" she was trying to be mindful of her volume, but she also needed him to hear her. "Is everything okay?"

Still nothing from the other side of the door.

Cecelia tried the knob and found it to be unlocked. She slowly pushed open the door and poked her head inside.

Max was on the floor, back against the wall facing the toilet, legs pulled up to his chest. There were tears running down his face, but he didn't seem to be crying. It was as if it were just happening to him, rather than something that he was consciously doing. He didn't look up as she walked into the bathroom and kneeled down in front of him.

Cecelia met his eyes, but there was no recognition there. He was staring right through her, unblinking. Cee reached out to him, wrapping her hands around his wrists and squeezing lightly.

"Max? What's going on? Are you feeling okay?" She reached for his face, pressing her hand against his forehead. He was much warmer than she remembered him being earlier in the day, possibly feverish, but she was desperately trying not to jump ahead of the situation.

"Can you hear me, Max? Can you feel my hands?" She held his head in her hands, feeling the heat coming off of him and trying to bring him back from wherever his mind was at the moment. He didn't seem to be hallucinating, which would've been a red flag.

She held her hand to his heart and found it to be beating rapidly.

"Max, if you can hear me, I'm just going to grab my phone. I'll be right back, just ten seconds and I'll be right back."

Cecelia ran to the living room and grabbed her cell off of the coffee table. She wasn't going to dial 911 just yet, but if Max didn't come to within the next half hour then she thought she might have to.

From the way he was acting, or not acting, Cee was pretty sure that Max was in the middle of a full-blown panic attack. It seemed to have paralyzed him for the moment, but he would be fine. Or at least well enough to respond to her, even if it was just a nod.

Cecelia rushed back into the bathroom and grabbed a washcloth. She let the cool water run over it and rang it out before folding it neatly and putting it to Max's forehead. She lifted it and softly blew cool air on the spot she'd just wet before moving on to his right cheek.

"You're going to be okay, Max," she kept her voice calm and low. "Just focus on the cold water and the cool air. Just breathe. In and out, you're going to feel so much better. Just a few more minutes."

There were no longer any tears coming from his eyes, but his pupils were still dilated, his eyes dead. Cecelia moved the cloth to the back of his neck, meeting Max's eyes just inches from his face.

"Look at me, Max. I'm right here, listen to my voice and look at me. I'm right here."

Cecelia could feel her own stomach starting to clench, the nerves she'd been fighting off starting to get the better of her.

"Please, Max. Look at me. I'm right here," she was trying

her best not to plead, not to let too much emotion into her own voice. He needed her calm and she would be that for him.

She let her head drop for just a second, breathing deeply and regaining her composure. When her eyes moved back to Max's face, he was looking back at her.

"Hey, can you hear me?" She kept the rag at the back of his neck, aware that it had probably grown warm from the heat of his skin by now.

Max nodded slowly, moving his hand up to rub at his damp face.

"What am I doing in here, Cee? Did I get sick again?" his voice sounded as if he'd spent the whole day screaming at the top of his lungs, it was that raw. She knew he hadn't spoken more than a few words in the past three days.

"I don't think so. I heard you get up so I came to see if you were all right and I found you like this. You don't remember getting out of bed?"

Max shook his head, "I don't."

"It's okay, you're okay, just a little confusion. It's completely normal," Cecelia stood slowly, placing the washcloth in the sink behind her and reached her hands down towards Max. "Come on, let's get you back to bed."

Cecelia found the sheets to be sweat soaked, so she did a quick swap before letting Max crawl back in. It was getting late and she was exhausted from the past few days. She knew that she wouldn't get much sleep, but she wanted to at least try.

She'd been sleeping on the couch, giving Max some space and banking on the fact that, while he could possibly sneak out of bed quite easily, it would be harder for him to unchain and open the heavy door to her apartment without her hearing if she were out here.

Tonight, though, she thought she might lay with him for a while. There was something about the look on his face as he pulled the covers closer to his chest. She didn't want him to be alone, and she certainly didn't want to be far from him after what had just happened.

She crawled into the bed, the fresh sheets giving a false sense of tranquility, and curled into him as the tears began to fall from her eyes. And he didn't reach for her, he couldn't even look at her, he just whispered. *I'm sorry, I'm sorry, I'm sorry.* And there were tears rolling from his eyes, too, she noticed.

Cecelia reached her arms above her head in a deep stretch, stifling a yawn and opening her eyes against the weak slivers of light coming through the blinds in her bedroom. She'd fallen asleep after all and, from the looks of it, spent the entire night dead to the world. She glanced over at Max, checking to see if he'd had as restful a night as she did, but the spot beside her was empty.

Cecelia slammed her feet to the floor, rushing out of her room and into the bathroom. The door cracked loudly against the wall as she swung it open, but there was no sign of him there. How could she be so stupid? She should've just gone back to the couch when she felt her eyes drifting shut.

As she rounded the corner into her small living room, she found Max sound asleep in the spot where she'd spent the past two nights. He was wearing the same clothes he'd been in last night and his shoes were nowhere in sight. She leaned over to check his breathing before heading back into her bedroom.

His sneakers and jacket were in the same spot they'd been since he came over three days ago, thrown haphazardly near her closet. It didn't look like he'd snuck out, but she wouldn't know for sure until she talked to him. Even then, he would never admit to it. Cecelia could feel tears of frustration biting at her eyes. If the past three days had been for nothing she'd lose it.

Max didn't wake up for four hours and, while Cecelia was happy that he was getting some much needed rest, all it did was give her time to think up a million worst case scenarios in her mind.

He snuck out in the middle of the night to buy drugs. He knew she'd check his things, so he called his dealer and had him come over here, which then meant a drug dealer had her address. He ran downstairs in his t-shirt and boxers to meet his dealer at the apartment complex door, effectively letting all of her neighbors know what was going on. She shook her head.

She'd taken the opportunity go through his phone while he slept and found nothing incriminating on it. Didn't mean he hadn't deleted the call or text, but Cee had no evidence and no reason to think that Max had even tried anything. But why was he out here and would he really pass up the opportunity to get a quick fix while Cecelia slept?

Cecelia settled herself in the cozy armchair across from the couch that Max was on, just waiting for him to wake up. Willing him to wake up. It took forever, but when he finally cracked his eyes open it was to find Cecelia peering expectantly at him from across the room. As if he'd fallen asleep mid-question and she'd waited all this time for his answer.

"Cee?" his voice was garbled from sleep and exhaustion and probably a million other things.

"Why are you on the couch, Max? Why didn't you just stay in the bed?" She knew she sounded a bit unhinged, but who could blame her? She was beginning to crack under the pressure of this whole ordeal and the past few hours had done a world of damage to an already weak foundation.

"I puked in the bed, Cee," Max seemed confused by his own statement. "Didn't I? I remember waking up to throw up near my face. I think it was mostly on my pillow so I threw that in the tub, but there's definitely a little bit on the sheets too. I didn't want to wake you up, though. I know you needed the sleep."

Cecelia didn't respond to him. She checked the bathroom, noting the pillow she hadn't noticed before and the foul smell that accompanied it. She'd brushed her teeth in here and everything. If she weren't so worried about Max, she would seriously be doubting her own sanity right now.

Sure enough, there were a few small spots of vomit on Max's side of the bed. Not enough to smell up the room, but enough that she'd need to wash the sheets and scrub at the mattress a bit. Maybe she should run out and grab one of those plastic mattress covers that parents use for bed wetters, that was sure to boost Max's confidence. Cecelia laughed to herself at that. Yes, she was definitely losing her mind in here.

Cecelia stripped the bed and went back to the living room, where Max didn't seem to have moved an inch.

"Did you do anything else last night, Max?"

She felt like she'd found lipstick on the collar of his shirt and was trying to corner him into a confession. But, she figured, if he did sneak out last night then that was just the same as cheating on her.

Max looked thoughtful for a second.

"After I threw up, I went to the bathroom and brushed my teeth and then I had some water. I think I walked around the living room a few times, just to stretch my legs a little. I haven't really been using them lately. It felt nice to move around, but then I felt bad again and really tired, so I laid down on the couch. And now we're here."

"That's it? Just some water and a walk."

"Cecelia, I didn't go anywhere else. I promise you. I thought of it, but I didn't do it. I wanted to, but I swear that I didn't," he looked so sincere, but she never could be sure.

"Please don't lie to me, Max," she hoped he could tell how sad it made her to speak to him this way, that she got no pleasure from asking these questions.

"I'm not, I know you have no reason to trust me, but I didn't do anything. I don't even know where my phone is right now."

"I hope for your own sake that you're telling the truth, Max," she stood from the chair she'd taken. "This sucks for me, I know that you know that, but it's your life on the line, not mine."

Max nodded solemnly before lying back down and stretching out along the couch. He was asleep again within minutes.

Day four seemed to be the turning point, which was on par with most of what Cecelia had read. Max seemed to be doing okay. He wasn't in any visible pain and his demeanor had changed drastically from the night before. He even smiled at her a little when she brought some toast and Gatorade into bed for him to snack on. And that half smile made her heart jump.

She'd been so focused and so very stressed that she hadn't really thought about what it would be like when things started to smooth out for them. To her, that quirk of his lips may very well be the beginning of their future.

Because, yes, they'd been together for over three years at this point and, yes, they were as fully committed as any other couple she knew, but the past week had changed things. It was the most intense thing she'd ever been through and they'd done it together. She'd stayed strong for him and he'd stuck it out for her. There was a maturity in this whole experience that she hadn't seen coming. And, hell, if that didn't bring a new warmth to her heart.

And so, very tentatively, she suggested a movie. And very softly, Max said sure. And Cecelia took that opportunity to snuggle into Max's side and drape her arm across his stomach just because she finally could. The horror had passed and, though there was still work ahead, she would allow herself this moment to breathe.

CHAPTER 13

2015
May

Cecelia walked to her desk on Monday morning with a smile, fresh iced coffee in hand. She waved to coworkers she'd seen just last week as if she hadn't seem them in years, the gratitude she felt at finally being out of her cramped apartment rushing through her. The sadness and anxiety of the past few days had taken flight for the moment, leaving her room to breathe, free from checking pulses and listening at doors.

Max had gone back to his parents' house, telling them great tales of the awful flu that had taken both he and Cee down, she was sure. She wasn't foolish enough to think they were completely out of the woods yet, she felt confident that the hardest part of this whole process was behind them. At least for her. It was up to Max now to keep his demons at bay. Cecelia shook that thought from her mind. That was a worry for later, right now she was a normal girl, opening emails and sipping on a coffee, passing the hours until she could clock out for the day.

Lou had called and asked her to grab a drink after work and she'd happily agreed. She'd never needed her friend more and even if she couldn't tell her about the week she'd just had, being near Lou was sure to make her feel the same comfort that she always felt just from catching up and having a laugh.

It's so difficult to put into words all of the ways that your friends end up saving you. How their successes have spurred your successes, how their positivity has helped you to maintain your own, how they're kindness has made you kinder. It's such a potent admiration, and one Cecelia wholeheartedly hoped was returned.

Since it was a nice night, they'd opted for a drink on the pier in Hoboken. It was a quick drive from Cee's apartment, though they'd decided to Uber after taking the PATH in from the city, and they'd both agreed that they'd rather get out of the city after work rather than combat the happy hour crowd in midtown.

As they carried their bucket of sangria over to two open beach chairs, Cee couldn't help but notice that Lou seemed extra excited about something. Luckily for Cecelia, Lou was as anxious to get to the point as Cee was curious to hear it.

"So, I have something fun to tell you," Lou lead in.

"I can see that. Spill!"

"I hope you're ready for a new roommate because I just got promoted," and it was hands down the best thing Lou could've said that day.

"YES!" Cecelia jumped out of her chair, nearly spilling her glass of sangria, and gave Lou a bone-crushing hug. "I'm so happy for you! Six months and you're already killing it! This is so awesome!"

"I know, right? I was so surprised, but I really have been working my ass off. It just feels nice that someone noticed," Lou was beaming.

"You have no idea, Lou. This is the best news I've heard in a long time," Cee grabbed her wallet out of her person and stood. "You stay here and bask in your successful day, I'm getting another pitcher. This night just turned into a celebration."

And with that, they split not two, but three bottles of sangria and talked all about the adorable decorations they'd get for the apartment and the healthy meals they'd cook and the gym classes they'd attend and, to Cecelia, this step forward felt like a piece of her past coming back to her and she couldn't be more grateful for it. Lou was moving in and Max was getting better and things might actually be okay.

Cee called Max as soon as she got home and told him all about her wonderful news and he congratulated her in the sweet way that he sometimes spoke when he was feeling extra proud to be with her. And she knew his happiness wasn't just for her, it was for himself too. Because she'd stuck by him and he still had her and even the absolute ugliest part of him was still worth it to her.

CHAPTER 14

2015
May – June

Cecelia called her landlord the very next day and he agreed to let her move from her one bedroom apartment to a two bedroom on the floor above. Louisiana moved in at the start of September and it was so nostalgic to see her parents carrying boxes into the apartment and so exciting to start this new chapter of adulthood, which she knew would be one of the last before she took the leap with Max and they found their own place together. It was a nostalgic step forward for Cee.

Timing really was everything, she thought to herself as she propped herself up on Lou's newly assembled bed and gave her a 'yes' or 'no' as she unpacked the bins that had carried her clothes from her parents home to this one. Lou was trying to eliminate anything too "college-y" from her wardrobe, a mission which left many a spandex skirt and sequin top in the donation pile.

Had Lou gotten this promotion a month earlier, Cecelia wouldn't have been able to do what she had for Max. There was no hiding what was going on, and, even if she could get away with calling it the flu, Cecelia was a terrible liar. She'd never be able to keep something like that from Lou, not if she had to explain it to her face to face.

It felt like pieces falling into place, like an instant reward for taking on Max's burden as her own and putting her own life aside to help him battle through. That, and the fact that Max had very slowly started talking about using his degree.

He couldn't do much at the moment with a solo psychology degree, but putting in a few more years of schooling would change that. Cecelia had been pushing for a law degree, even taking it upon herself to research some schools that were within commuting distance.

He'd ended up with a psychology degree when the business major he'd been pursuing didn't pan out. He couldn't keep up with the classes, and he realized junior year that, with the gen eds and electives he'd already taken, he could still graduate on time if he switched to the psych program.

He'd fallen into the major and never took it the step further that he needed to.

It took her a few weeks, but Cecelia eventually convinced him to just take the LSAT and see how it went. He would need to take the test now if he wanted to get any applications in for the following fall semester, and there was no harm in trying. Max agreed, as he tended to do these days, and they'd studied. She helped him pick out the books he would need and she quizzed him and watched as his confidence grew.

There was a renewed purpose to him now, a goal to work toward. When the time for the test finally came, Max seemed almost excited to take it. As if he knew he would pass and couldn't wait to finally celebrate something, to earn back the respect that those closest to him had inevitably lost over the past few months.

His score wasn't perfect, but it was more than enough to qualify him for many of the schools they'd been eyeing. The smile that he'd worn after that was like nothing Cecelia had seen out of him. And she couldn't tell if it was because his cheeks had finally started to fill back out or because his eyes had finally lost the dull glaze that she'd grown accustomed to, but Max was more handsome then she ever remembered.

"Wow, I can't believe it. You're actually going to be a lawyer. My boyfriend, a tall, handsome lawyer. How did I ever get so lucky?" Cecelia was snuggled into Max's side in bed, laughing into his chest at her own comments.

"Let's not get too far ahead of ourselves, Cee," Max was propped up against her headboard, reading through his results again. "I have to get accepted into a school first."

"You will, though. Your scores are good, Max. It's all going to work out."

"We'll see. I don't even know where I want to apply yet," she knew he must have every word in this document memorized by now, but he was still reviewing it as if he was missing the joke somewhere.

"Well, I have a few ideas if you want to hear them," she smiled at the amused sigh he let out. She couldn't just enjoy this success for one night; she was already a million miles ahead of him.

"Shoot."

"Okay, so I know I already mentioned Seton Hall and I definitely think that should stay on the list. It's a great school and it's so convenient to get to. But," she lifted herself on to her elbow and met his eyes excitedly, "What about Rutgers?"

"Back to the old stomping grounds?" Max seemed to brighten up at the thought of heading back to the campus where they'd met.

"Not exactly. The law school is on the Newark campus, which is so, so close and I could even take the train and meet you after work. We could get dinner in the Ironbound or see shows at Prudential. It would be so much fun."

"A Rutgers man through and through?" Max questioned her.

"Exactly."

"Kind of like a Harvard man, but not quite?"

"Hey, you're from New Jersey. A Rutgers man is our Harvard man."

"Okay, you've got yourself a deal. I'll apply, but we have about a year to kill before I start anywhere so maybe we should focus this brainstorm session on the nearer future."

"I actually have an idea about that too."

"You're an insane person."

"Shush, Max. I'm just excited for you. So excited, that I had Lou talk to her Aunt Layla. She runs her own law firm in Montclair and she offered to take you on as an assistant around the office. That way you can get some firsthand experience."

"Seriously?"

"Seriously. I'm not sure what the pay will be, but you can still keep your weekend shifts at Central if need be. It's just for the next few months until you get accepted somewhere."

"Cee, I don't deserve you. You know that right?"

"Stop that. I just want us to both be happy and I think having this will do that for you. You deserve that, don't you think?"

"I think I'm very lucky," he leaned down and planted a kiss on her head. "Get your shoes on, I'm taking you out for dinner tonight to celebrate. Wherever you want."

As Cecelia pulled on her boots, she glanced over at Max. She'd always loved him and been proud of him, but this just took the cake. There was just something so sexy about this decision, about Max in this serious light. She could feel the excitement in her stomach already at what the night held and, even more so, at what the life ahead of them held.

Looking back, Max probably spent about as much time responding to her sexts as he did researching all of the many notes that Layla would give him throughout the day. It felt like role play for a minute there, and she was fine with being the criminal or the judge or even the freaking stenographer as long as she found herself in the courtroom with him, watching him pretend to be this all-important, hard ass lawyer, charming the pants off the jury and his girlfriend all at the same time.

And it became nearly impossible to connect this man, this thriving version of him, to the way he'd been just a few months earlier. She just couldn't believe that he was the same person. And she couldn't deny the pride she'd felt in the fact that she'd helped him get here. Because maybe his parents or

ALLYSON SOUZA

his friends would've caught on and stepped in, or maybe they wouldn't have and he would be skin and bones again, or, even worse, maybe just bones.

CHAPTER 15

2015
July – August

It wasn't long before Max was finally filling out applications and readying himself for interviews, should the offers come. Cecelia spent Max's application hours filling out a few of her own. She wasn't sure how long it would take her to find a new position and she wanted to give herself a head start. She knew that she'd told Lou she was planning on waiting a year, but she couldn't fathom spending a second longer than that in pharmaceutical writing.

In July she finally got an offer, just as Max accepted a spot in the program at Rutgers to start in the fall. She'd be a content writer at an up and coming website and, though she didn't love the fluffy, filler pieces that she'd be working on, she was so pumped to put this on her resume and see where it could take her after she paid her dues.

Max took her out to celebrate on her first day and they walked along the water and made love back at her place and it was all so *good*. But, there was always a chance that the other shoe could drop. She knew this. She would watch him sometimes, with wary eyes, as he lost sleep over an exam or got into a mood about a bad grade. She was looking for the signs she'd missed before, because she thought, if anything drags him back, it will be this.

She could see him feeling inadequate and frustrated and in need of something to make him feel better. And she tried to be that thing, but she had her own life, too. She was trying to impress her new boss and juggle a new schedule and she couldn't spend all day worried about if Max was going to fall back into old habits.

It was also really difficult to get mad or spit out accusations, when all you felt was gratitude. When faced with the loss of someone, it becomes second nature to cherish that person that much more. So if Max snapped at her, or canceled plans, or forgot to ask her about her day, she found herself more forgiving than she maybe should have been. The scales had been tipped and she found herself off balance. Why be mad when she could stay thankful? Why cause a problem when she still had Max in front of her?

So she observed him, she Googled signs and symptoms, she watched and she waited. Because, she hadn't realized it until just then, but she really didn't have any trust in him when it came to this. She thought he'd proven himself, but all he did was go through withdrawals and who knew what happened after that? He could've gone right back and just hidden it better. He could've switched drugs and she wouldn't even know what to look for.

And it was a scorching hot August day when she found him, back turned, swallowing a pill in her apartment kitchen. He'd run across the street to grab a pack of Gatorade from the convenience store, walked right into the kitchen, tilted his head back in that oh so familiar way and fucked up the whole trajectory of their lives.

"Max?" her voice was weak, she could barely get his name off her lips.

"Yeah, babe?" he turned to look at her then and his face fell. She'd seen him. "Cecelia, it's not what it looks like."

"Shut the fuck up, Max," she was rushing into her bedroom then, grabbing for her purse, her wallet, her jacket. Check, check, check.

"Cee, please just wait. I'm sorry, okay. I'm really sorry. I promise this isn't an issue. I just fucked up, it's not like it was before," and his eyes were pleading with her to just listen, to just believe him. But she couldn't. Not after the hell she'd been through last time.

"Get out of my way. Right now," she couldn't handle this. They were supposed to be meeting her parents for lunch in fifteen minutes. She was going to tell them about a story she'd written that week. It had been the highest viewed piece her site had put out that week and her supervisor told her no one had ever claimed that spot in the few weeks that it took her to do so.

"Cee, come on. Let's just go meet your parents. We can talk about this later," He was trying to reason with her, but he was patronizing and it was just so fucking stupid at this point.

"*I'm* going to meet my parents. Looks like you came down with the flu again, Max. Pity, I'm sure my mom would've loved to have seen you," and with that Cecelia stormed out of the apartment with angry tears streaming down her face.

Her parents were worried when she'd shown up alone and so upset, so she dropped the flu story and just told them that she and Max had gotten into a huge fight. The kind of fight that might just end the whole damn thing.

"I'm sure it isn't that bad, honey. You'll talk it out when you get back, but for now it's probably good for both of you to cool off," her mom's voice was soothing to her in any tone, but this one was especially calming.

She could already feel her shoulders relaxing. This had happened so many times in her life when things were going badly for her. It was as if just spending time with her mom and dad brought her back to the basics, reminded her of what she had no matter what else was blowing up around her. Her family would be here and, if Max wasn't, then that would be enough.

"Thanks, mom. You're probably right. I don't even want to talk about it and risk it ruining our afternoon. Is Sedona going to meet us later?"

"I think she might. She was at Lauren's house swimming,

but she said that she'd walk over after if we get dessert."

"Seriously? I haven't seen her in weeks and all she cares about is dessert?"

"You know her, she's all caught up in her friends. This is the last month they have before people start leaving for college."

"Yeah, wouldn't want to force family time when they've got comforters and dorm posters to choose," her dad added with a smirk. He always had this glint in his eye when he talked about his daughters, as if everything they did was the most amusing thing in the whole world.

If he'd have preferred sons to the two girls he got, you'd never know. Of course, he was probably a bit more excited for the soccer games he'd attended over the years than the dance recitals, but he was front and center for each and every event regardless.

There hadn't been a single time that Cecelia looked for him over the years that he wasn't standing there, arms crossed, silently supporting her and she owed him for that. And, sitting there, she realized he'd probably murder someone if he knew the heaviness that Max was bringing to her world.

The three of them ordered pizza and a round of beers, because why not, and they caught up on everything. Her mom told her about a party that her aunt was throwing for Labor Day and her dad asked her about work, which reminded her of the forgotten story and the new career milestone she'd just hit. And the smile that they shared, that "look what we did" show of pride, was enough to totally erase Max from her mind for the rest of the afternoon. She would be fine.

Max was sitting at the desk in her bedroom when she got back to the apartment. He seemed to be working on something, maybe one of the assignments of Layla's that he hadn't gotten to that week, but she could tell by the slump in his shoulders that he was probably just staring at the paper in front of him. At least he was upset about what happened. She'd have killed him if she came back and he was watching the game or playing on his phone.

"Hey," she said it quietly as she shrugged off her jacket and hung it on the hook near the door.

"Hey, you're back. How was lunch?"

"Max, please don't act like nothing happened."

"Did I ever thank you? After the last time," this subject change threw her. She'd been gearing up for another version of the same old fight.

"I don't know, Max. It wasn't really the kind of situation that requires a thank you. I felt like you agreeing to go through it was thanks enough."

"That's bullshit," he turned fully around now, so he could face her head on. "I should've been on my knees thanking you every single day. You saved my life, Cee. I was in such bad shape and you just refused to let me get any worse. It's the best thing anyone's ever done for me and I didn't even say thanks."

"What's the point of this, Max? You didn't thank me, it's not a big deal. I didn't buy you a present, I was just doing what anyone would've done in the same situation."

"That's not true. A lot of girls would've just said screw this and jumped ship. Hanging around isn't the only option."

"I'm in love with you, it was the only option for me."

"I love you, too. You know that right? You know I love you more than anything in the whole world?"

"Yeah, Max, I do."

"So, when this shit happens, when I slip up and I make these huge mistakes, you know I do it in spite of the fact that I have you? This has nothing to do with you. I have a personal problem and it's ruining things for you."

"Max, you're scaring me. What are you trying to say?"

"I'm trying to tell you that I lied. That wasn't a one-time thing in the kitchen earlier," he dropped his face into his hands at that. "I'm such a piece of shit."

"How long?" Her voice was soft again and she really wished that she could force some power into it.

"About two weeks after I went through the withdrawals

last time," his voice, while shaky, was clear. He'd spent her time out with her parents preparing for this.

"Damn it."

"I know. I'm sorry. I'm so sorry. I thought I could get it back under control and I don't think I can. Not alone. I couldn't do it on my own last time, I don't know why I thought it would be any different now."

"Okay, so what do you want to do? Do you want to look into rehabs? Do you want to see a doctor?"

"I don't know. I don't think I should even be the person to make that decision."

She stared at him for a few seconds, just taking in his face and his eyes and his mouth. Just looking at this man who seemed so like a stranger sometimes, but so much like a part of her own body at others.

"I know it's a lot to ask, but we've done it before and I don't want to be like this anymore. I have so much more to lose now. I know you're not going to stay with me if I keep doing this and I know I can't keep my grades up if I let this happen again. So please, will you help me?"

Still, she couldn't find an answer for him. He reached for her, taking her hands in his, holding on.

"It's a story, Cee and I've been telling it for years. It starts with me saying I'm fine and it hasn't ended yet so I can't tell you about that. But looking at you right now, I'm scared that I'm about to find out. Don't tell me how it ends. I'm begging you to stay in the beginning of the story with me. Because that's where we are. This is the beginning. I want decades with you. I want to pull you out of bed when we're 80, even if it hurts my back and cracks my bones. There's a plan here and I know that I've been fucking it up, but that's how stories get told. This is the low point and if we just stay together we can get to the good stuff. Please, don't let me know how it ends. Please, Cee.

I'm learning to fight this for real. I have it in me, I know I can do it and I can be a real person and stop wasting money killing myself. It doesn't have to be this way. It won't always be this way. Just give me one more chance, I promise you that I will never touch another pill again. I know what I have to lose and I can't lose you. I can't be apart from you and know that I ruined it for us."

And though they hadn't said any vows, she understood this as the part of their commitment where for better or worse came into play. And she loved him in the way that made those vows seem applicable, though they'd never spoken them to one another. She felt them in her bones when she looked at him and heard his voice and felt him lean towards her in random moments of closeness.

For years, she planned to say them to him one day and she promised herself now that she would live by them as practice so that her life may one day be the way she so badly wanted it to be. With the two of them in a home of their own, falling into step with one another as they made breakfast together or brushed their teeth at night. With him lifting her through a doorway and carrying her to bed, laying her down, and creating a new life in their own right.

And if Max wasn't the one she ended up with, she felt bad for the man that was. Because this wasn't going away. She felt it even as she agreed to stay, as she let him pull her into his arms and rested his weary head against hers. This was her man, this was her choice and if he forced her to walk a different path she would hold onto both love and hate for him. She would always dream of the life that she could have had.

CHAPTER 16

2015
August

And so they did it again. Cecelia was too new at her job to be taking vacation already, so the next week she called out sick on Friday and Monday, giving them four days together. She remembered him feeling at least slightly better after the third day last time, so she figured it'd be all right to do it this way.

And it was just as awful as she remembered. It made no difference that he'd come to her this time, and that it had been his decision, rather than her forcing him to do it. That mental fortitude didn't carry over into these days and nights of pain and sickness. She didn't even tell anyone she was sick this time. Her parents wouldn't notice that she wasn't going to work and the only other person who'd wonder why she wasn't heading into the city would be Louisiana.

She couldn't exactly hide it from her roommate, so she told her everything. And it felt so damn good to have someone on her side, to let someone into this terrible little world that she'd been dealing with since the year before. She could see that Lou really didn't know how to respond, and that was okay. She just didn't want her to feel uncomfortable in the apartment, but Lou was much more worried about the toll that this would take on Cecelia. And to that, all Cecelia could say was that it had been lessened an unbelievable amount now that she had Lou to talk to.

And she did just that. At the end of each day, with Max tucked away in her bed, Cecelia made sure that she ate dinner with Lou. It gave her a false sense of normalcy and it was so nice to be able to give someone an update on Max. Even if she just threw out a quick, "Things are better today," it made her feel less alone.

It wasn't until a week after she'd told Lou, when Max had already gotten back on his feet and gone back to his parents' house for a few days, that Lou finally sat Cecelia down.

"Listen, Cecelia. I'm not going to ever tell you what to do, or judge you for making a decision I don't understand, but I feel like I need to say something here," Lou began, and Cee braced herself. It was rare to see Louisiana this serious about anything.

"This situation is serious. Like, life or death serious," Lou continued and Cee just nodded. "I think that you should involve Max's family. Even if it's just letting his sister know so that she can keep an eye at him when he's home. I know that we aren't kids anymore and it might feel weird to go to his parents, but I'm not sure that this is something you should be doing alone."

"I know, Lou. I totally understand where you're coming from and I've been tempted so many times to do just that, but I just don't know how much it could possibly help. From the very vague history of this whole mess that I've gotten from Max, his family knows about this and has tried to help him before. I think at this point they'd just send him away to some rehab and he really, really, doesn't want that."

"Should that be up to him, though? He's clearly got a lot going on right now, I can't imagine that he's thinking clearly at all. He needs someone to step in, he needs real help, Cecelia."

"And what have I been doing, Lou? I'm trying my best to get him through this in a way that he's comfortable with. He doesn't want to go to rehab, he doesn't think it'll help him and, from what I've been reading, he might be right," And now Cecelia could feel hear the emotion in her own voice, could feel her hands start to get that slight shake that signaled tears or an explosion of some sort.

"It's a bubble, Lou. He'd go away for a month and spend time in an environment that we could never recreate, that we could never offer him here and he'd get clean and then he'd come back and there goes his safe little world. And then his tolerance is low and his craving comes back and that's when shit could really get bad. Do you know how many people overdose as soon as they get home from rehab? It's sick. And I can't have that happen. I couldn't survive that. So he needs to do it here. He needs to do it on his own terms in the world he lives in or it won't stick. I'm not being stupid, Louisiana, I'm doing everything I can and it's been a million times easier for me since I told you. Please, just be here for me and trust that I'm doing the best thing for him. I love him more than anything in the whole world and I'm truly doing what I think will save him."

And the saddest look was resting on Lou's face when Cecelia finally finished her little speech. "Okay, Cee," she shrugged, "I'm here for you, always. I trust you. I just want you to be okay. I don't want this to start dragging you down, too."

"I know and I love you for that, but we're going to get through this and Max will graduate and it will all be okay. And, if it starts to feel like more than I can take, then I promise to find another way. I love him, but I love me, too and I won't forget it."

And Cecelia wrapped her very best friend up in her arms and hugged her hard, hoping that Lou wouldn't let this affect them. That she wouldn't start to lose her in helping Max.

It wasn't until the next week that Cecelia's life finally took a turn for the better. She'd walked to her cubicle on a Wednesday morning, iced latte in hand and her favorite pair of heels on her feet. Her day got off to an average start, she spent the morning answering emails and working on her next article, which was going well so far.

She convinced her favorite coworker Lita to grab lunch in Bryant Park, and they'd spent that hour sipping on fancy iced teas and talking about their bosses and the group of tourists two tables over who seemed to have gotten terribly drunk at noon on a Wednesday.

It was when Cecelia came back to her desk to find a note from her boss that the day began to take its true shape. Because this day, as it were, would turn out to be very important in the grand scheme of things. It was a rare starting point, when things begin to unravel and there's nothing that you can do to stop them.

Stan's note had instructed her to meet him in his office at 3 pm for a short meeting. Cecelia spent the hour prior to this meeting going through her emails and her calendar and anything she could get her hands on that might prepare her for whatever it was that Stan wanted to talk about.

At 55 years old, Stan Gilport was a stout and friendly man who'd been great to Cecelia since the day she started this job. He seemed to truly believe that she was a talented writer and, though critique was necessary, he also took the time to tell her when he enjoyed an article and to compliment her work whenever he felt that she was doing well.

So she was more curious than nervous when she lightly knocked on Stan's office door that warm Wednesday afternoon at 3 pm sharp. Stan called her in and told her to have a seat as he pulled a sheet of paper from a pile on his desk. He didn't hand it to her right away though. Instead, he seemed to study her for a moment.

"I'm not totally sure about what I'm about to say, but I have a gut feeling about it and, as soon as I saw the piece of paper I knew that I needed to have this conversation with you."

"Okay," and, as always, she tried to ensure that she sounded confident. It didn't matter that she had no idea what was going on, she wanted her boss to know that she was ready for it.

"I'll get to the point. So basically, the company is hosting a competition of sorts, beginning next week, and I want you to enter. I think you'll win, without a doubt in my mind." He slid the sheet of paper he'd been holding across his desk to Cecelia.

She took a second to read it, then shook her head.

"Creative writing? Stan, that's not really what I do."

"I know it isn't your job right now, but, I'm sorry if this offends you, I feel like you're wasting your talent. You've got a real voice, your work is so engaging and, yes, there can be improvements made here and there, but you're a good writer and that's the bottom line. I watched every other editor in there turn up their nose at this and I think they're being ignorant. I want to get ahead of this."

"But the site doesn't even publish fiction. I don't understand."

"It's something new that the higher ups are trying to get off the ground. Once a month, they'd like to publish a short story that follows some sort of relevant theme. They'd like the website to have more of a voice, a bit more personality, if you will, and I want it to be your voice."

"If you want me to enter, of course I'll enter. I'm just not sure that I can do this style as well as you think I can."

"I know you can do it. I'm your editor, remember? There's no one else on this staff who can write the way you do. And that's not to say there aren't other talented people here, everyone here is excellent at what they do, but I don't believe that they can do this. And I don't think their editors will be encouraging them to do it, either. If you win, it's essentially a complete role change, but it would be a sort of promotion. You'd be the head of this little sector and it would give you more stability here. No one's numbers to compete with, no having to give a story up because someone pitched it five minutes before you. You'd have complete freedom."

"Okay, yes. Yes, I'm going to do this. Thanks, Stan. Really, this sounds like an awesome opportunity and I probably wouldn't have given it a second thought without your encouragement."

"Good, great, Cecelia. Here, take the paper with you. The terms are pretty clear, but let me know if you have any questions. And I'm with you on this, to bounce ideas off of or to read drafts, just let me know."

"Thanks, Stan. I better get back to my desk, but I'm going to go through all of this tonight."

"Me too, Cecelia. For the first time in maybe ten years this company is doing something I'm really excited about."

Cecelia hurried back to her desk, popped in her headphones so she wouldn't be bothered, and ate up every word on the form that Stan had given her. She really never would've thought of herself for this type of thing, but Stan had done a good job in convincing her that she could do it. And it really seemed simple enough.

Every two weeks, prospective applicants (the info sheet was avoiding calling this a contest, it was being pitched as a long, in-company application process) would submit a short story, 5,000 words or less that had to do with something relevant in their own lives.

They were instructed to give honest accounts of their struggles, relationships, travels, anything that would interest or inspire their peers. Of course, the stories were supposed to be fiction, so they would have to maintain that style, but it seemed like she could write word for word a fight that she and Max or she and Lou had had and just change the names. And it was in this moment that Cecelia's life really came into perspective for her.

Because all of the nice, normal girls her age would have pretty much the same thing to say. But she had something different, something powerful, to share. And it was fiction, so she wouldn't use their names or their location or any other identifying factors, but she knew that at least one of her submissions would detail the heartache that comes with addiction, even when you aren't the addict. And the fear, she would most definitely be including the fear.

Cecelia's first two article submissions were on the lighter side, which she'd done on purpose. She had a plan to slowly build to her deeper entries and, she figured, it would be better to write about the more serious topics after she'd gotten some feedback and allowed herself to get used to writing creatively in a way that she hadn't done since college. Submission comments were sent via email from a generic company address three days after entries were received and Cecelia was happy with the reaction she was getting so far.

Her comments were less about content and more about keeping the tone throughout and small grammar notes that seemed to be more editor preference than actual mistakes. Stan always read her stories beforehand, so she'd know if she was making any glaring errors before her work reached the top.

She was also working chronologically, beginning with the conversation she and her parents had the night before she left for college. They'd wanted to give her some advice, but it turned into an emotional night, including a few walks down memory lane and this insane feeling of her childhood really and truly slipping through her fingers for the first time.

Next, she'd hit on her first real fight with Louisiana. They'd been reading a magazine and Louisiana took it out of Cee's hands to read an article about sex. She'd made a comment about Cecelia not needing to see it because she was still a virgin and it just hit a nerve. She stormed out of the dorm room and didn't talk to Louisiana until she finally apologized two days later. It seemed petty now, but she was able to insert a lot of emotion into that one and she'd ended up being really pleased with the finished product.

For her next two, she planned on writing about the night she met Max and then she wanted to choose something from the months surrounding graduation. She wasn't sure if she was going to focus on the emotions leading up to leaving college or the stress of trying to get her bearings in the adult world, but she knew it would have something to do with that time in her life.

Finally, she would be writing about her discovery of Max's addiction and the subsequent withdrawals that she'd watched him go through. It was by far the darkest topic of the bunch and she thought that it might be straying too far into unknown territory as far as "experiences similar to her peers" went, but she was coming to realize that she may have taken this project on as an excuse to write it all down and to rationalize it that way.

She wasn't sure how it would turn out, but she knew that Max would read it and she wanted to be there when he did. She wanted to see his reaction just as much as she wanted to get a reaction out of him. Because he seemed to be able to spend four days nearly dying in bed and not speaking a word without ever bringing it up in conversation again, but she had a lot to say that she was too scared to mention.

She didn't want to be a trigger or to risk taking him back to that awful place when he was doing better, but it felt like she'd been through a silent war, and no one could really relate to the helplessness and the paralyzing fear that sat at the back of her mind day in and day out. Even now, she didn't feel truly sure that the problem was solved. Because she was so bad at recognizing the signs.

And this is where her fear really came from. Because maybe she'd never known him without this darkness hanging over him and maybe she would never see the signs because they were always there and had always *been* there. For as long as she'd known him he'd been like this and he seemed just the same to her now. And, as she began writing that last entry, as she let the crisp fall air wash over her at the end of October, she knew that she had been deluding herself.

A person doesn't just come off of a years-long addiction without a single part of his personality being affected. He'd be different, wouldn't he? If he really had stopped, wouldn't there be new habits or the loss of old ones? Wouldn't he be, essentially, a new man as she'd told him he would be each time he lay shaking in bed?

And, if he seemed so content staying exactly the same, she'd have to be the one to make some changes.

CHAPTER 17

2015
October – November

Max had asked her in September if she'd want to go away for her 24th birthday. It would fall on a Saturday this year, so he figured he could get all of his schoolwork done ahead of time and they could drive to Boston or somewhere around there for a few days and just be alone.

Cecelia hadn't known the mental state she'd be in when she agreed to this trip, but she was happy now, as she packed her bags, that she'd suggested just getting a little cabin in the Poconos and laying low for the weekend, rather than taking on a city. She filled up her duffel with sweaters and leggings and warm socks and she was sure that Max had stuck to a similar selection process.

They were bringing up frozen pizzas and hot chocolate and some beers with them, and there seemed to be a market near their cabin to grab eggs and milk and any essentials they'd need to get by. Max would be driving his old green Jeep up and Cecelia was happy to sit in the passenger seat and just observe him as the miles went by. He really was so handsome with his long nose and his strong jaw and that dark brown hair that curled just the slightest bit when it was overgrown, as it was now.

He'd been living like a hermit for the past few weeks, just

trying to survive law school. His workload was insane and he insisted on keeping his hours at the bar even though his parents had offered to help him financially until he reached graduation. His pale skin and his thin frame had a pit forming in her stomach. She'd reached for his hand then, and she'd held it for the remainder of the drive. She just wanted to be as close as she could get to him, to breathe him in every single second.

Max shot her a small smile as they reached the cabin and it took every ounce of strength in her not to burst out crying at that. Instead, she'd smiled back and kissed him soundly on the lips. They had the weekend and it would have to be enough for her.

As soon as they stepped into the cabin, she knew this would be good for them. This would be the perfect ending to their story, at least for the moment. There was a warmth that seemed to radiate from the walls, from the slouchy furniture laid out before them and the deep hues of the area rugs spread throughout the room. It came from the heavy drapes and the plush throw blankets scattered about.

It came from somewhere deep inside Cecelia that could only feel the importance of these impending moments. Max didn't know what this would come to represent for them, but it would be a good memory, something golden to hold on to. So Cecelia stepped inside and reached behind her for Max's hand. He shot her a lazy smile and she dragged him to her, pushed him past her, and she was on him the second the back of his knees hit the couch in front of them.

They made love everywhere that weekend, but it was this initial encounter that stuck with her the most vividly. There was something about the way that they didn't speak a word before or during or even for a long time after. It was the way her body felt when she was so close to him. It was just the comfort, really, of knowing that you're with the right person and that they're with the right person and you've created moments that no one can touch.

There would never be another man in another cabin in

another life that could do this to her. That could make her forget how awful everything actually was, forget that fact that it was all about to get so much worse. Yes, she was giving this up. She was about to walk away. But it wasn't with the hope of ever replacing Max.

It was with the hope that Max would stay somewhere in her heart forever and that she could access some fraction of this warmth from time to time. That she could get by and eventually find a different man to be there, to start something new with. But it wouldn't be this. This was once-in-a-lifetime. And she would put her hands on him and put her mouth on him and rest her head on him for as long as she could, until the very last second.

Cecelia woke on the couch with Max's arms wrapped around her, legs entangled, head in her hair. She found herself playing with his hands, tracing the outlines of his fingers on her stomach as she often did to wake him up. He tended to be a heavy sleeper, but this always seemed to irritate him enough to pull him back to her.

"Hey," it came as a whisper just behind her ear.

"Hey there, Sleeping Beauty," she whispered back.

He gripped the hands that had been playing with his and pushed a gentle kiss to the side of her head.

"What are you doing?"

"Just laying with you, you're so warm," she rolled towards him now, wrapping her arms around his neck.

He didn't answer, just kissed her.

"Are you hungry? We don't have anything to cook yet, but we could have some cereal," she wasn't very hungry herself, but she'd felt his stomach growl a time or two.

"I'm okay, I think we need to stay on the couch for now."

"We need to stay on the couch?"

"Yeah, this couch is the best part of the whole cabin, I wouldn't mind staying here the whole weekend. I like us on this couch."

"I like us here, too. Let's not move an inch."

"Well, I'm going to have to move just a little bit. Not off the couch, but to make optimal use of the couch there needs to be some changes made."

"Whatever you say, Max. You make those changes and I'll meet you there."

They were talking in between kisses at this point, hands everywhere. She was thanking God for the cushions below her and their width. They really *could* stay here all weekend. They really *should* stay here all weekend.

They didn't actually leave the couch until late Saturday morning, when they really couldn't ignore their rumbling stomachs any longer. They each had a bowl of dry cereal to hold them over until they could make the snowy drive down to the market and grab some real food.

They picked up the eggs and milk they needed for the rest of the weekend, with the plan to just whip up some easy meals. Pasta and mac and cheese would be on the menu and that was about it.

The small shop had been about six miles away from their cabin and the friendly older couple that owned it couldn't have been any sweeter. She envied them for a moment, as she watched Max pull $20 out of his wallet and pay for their goods. They'd grown old together, they had a peaceful life here in this small town and they had something to show for it. It was funny the things she'd come to admire as her relationship fell apart. It was sad to have to let them go.

Over the past few months, she'd tried to remember the signs of health, and to always have an eye out for them. Easy laughter, full cheeks, and flushed skin. She realized that she need not settle for one of three. It was all or nothing. And that realization led to nothing but more fear and, eventually, genuine panic.

And all of the talking, the honesty and the fighting side by side was in clear contrast with what she now knew to be true of addiction. She could support him every step of the way, every millisecond of every day, but she would never be on the battlefield with him. She would never feel his urges and let him tag her in, give him a break so he didn't have to fight *all the time*. This truly was his war, and she was no more than a bystander.

And if he wasn't strong enough to fight it, then she couldn't watch anymore. She had a life to live, without the constant worry. Without switching the radio station or turning off the news when a song or a report made her feel sensitive. There were people dying all around the country from the same thing that Max was doing. She hated that she now had a personal stake in it, that it all hit her so close to home when all she wanted to do was turn a blind eye.

She had work and family, she had friends that she hadn't seen in years, she needed to get back to all that. Max had become a recluse right before her eyes and now, it seemed, the same thing was happening with her. She went to work and she came home to see Max. She spent hours watching TV and reading books while he studied.

She should have been out with friends or visiting her parents or even heading to the movies solo as she used to do when she was younger, but she felt a pull towards him. She wanted to make sure someone was with him. Because God forbid something happened with him and she was out having a glass of wine. He could overdose; she'd known it since she first found out about all of this. And she was terrified of this fact. It was the most prominent thought on her mind most days and she could never seem to shake it.

And so she didn't. Instead, she dropped everything else and went to him. And it never really felt like she was giving anything else up. Sure, she'd love to take Louisiana up on her happy hour offers or join the girls for dinner one night, but would she even enjoy it? She would spend the whole night worrying, she'd be texting Max every second about absolutely nothing just to make sure he would respond. This is what it had all come to while she'd been too busy focusing on other things.

She couldn't live this way anymore. She loved him, but clearly there wasn't much she could do to help. She'd done the best that she could, short of admitting him into a rehab center. She thought of his parents, of their inability to solve this for him, but that couldn't stop her anymore.

And so she hurried back into the cabin with Max and they cooked themselves three boxes of mac and cheese to split for dinner. They snuggled up on the couch and talked about anything but themselves. They laughed about things that happened in college, they argued about how their favorite TV shows would end, they made out, they made love and then they fell asleep all tangled up.

When they woke up on Sunday morning they packed up and hit the road. They drove home in silence, Cecelia wrapping her fingers around Max's hand and holding on tight. The drive was beautiful, all snowy trees and icicles. The warmth of the heated car made it all so much more romantic, made it feel so much safer than it actually was. Because every second that passed had Cecelia feeling more and more like they should have never left the cabin.

The brakes on Max's jeep let out a sharp squeak as they slowed to a stop outside of Cee's apartment building. Cecelia tightened her grip on Max's hand, knowing he'd need it to shift the car into park, knowing he was about to pull it free.

"Do you know what my favorite thing about you is?" Her words came out in a rushed, nervous mess. Tripping over one another to reach Max.

"What's that?" He broke his hand away from hers, moved the gearshift and leaned back to get a better look at her. His tired eyes sparked with amusement, but just for a second. She nearly missed it in the darkness.

"My favorite thing about you is how you pull me in without reaching out. Sometimes you're just lying on the couch watching TV, you haven't even noticed me yet, you don't even realize there's pulling to be done, but, somehow, you're drawing me closer."

"Cee?" Max searched her face. "Why are you crying?"

"I just love you," she wasn't even bothering to wipe her

tears and Max remained still behind the wall she was raising between them.

"Cecelia, why are you crying?"

His voice was soft, quiet.

She could hear the anxiety starting to creep into his words and she wanted to talk to him about ownership in any and every form. She wanted to say to him whatever you do and whatever is done to you is yours and yours alone. We spend so much time trying to obtain things. It's all about what we want and what we can get, but we never seem to consider all that is simply handed to us.

"I'm scared of you. And for you. I don't trust you right now, and I think that you're maybe not doing as well as you say you are," he didn't respond, didn't seem able to, so she continued.

"I watch your eyes, I try to gauge your reactions to even the smallest comments, but I don't even have a reference point to compare them to because maybe you weren't yourself in the particular moment that I'm remembering. Maybe I've never seen you not high. I just need you to be honest with me, right now. Please tell me how you're doing, and please don't leave anything out."

"I don't know what you want me to say. We both know what's going on. If you need to hear it, I'll say it for you, but it's been nothing you haven't heard from me before. It's nothing I haven't crushed you with already over the past year."

"I don't need you to say it. I guess I just wanted to make sure we're both on the same page and that we agree on the fact that nothing's really changed. We haven't been able to do the things that we wanted to do or get to the place that we needed to get to."

"No, not yet. We're not there yet," she could tell he wanted to say more, that he understood going on the defensive was the only option now. But he also seemed to understand a step beyond that impulse.

"I can't do this anymore, Max," she didn't mean for it to be a whisper, but it was out there all the same.

"Cee," it was her name, she recognized that, but it sounded like a hiss of pain. As if he'd touched a hot pan. As if she'd burned him.

"I feel like you killed someone. I just can't figure out who it is. Most days it feels like me, but sometimes it feels like you," she was focused on a point just over his shoulder, on a dim street lamp casting shadows all through its domain.

"I never meant for it to be like this," he brought his hands to his head. "I never meant to do this to you."

"I know. I know that," she shrugged now, feeling the tears dripping from her chin.

"I'm sorry. I've never been so sorry in my life."

"I can't believe this is happening," she was wringing her hands together, white knuckled. "I can't believe I'm doing this."

"I gave you no choice. I want you to always remember that," he was crying openly now, but the look on his face was determined. "I gave you no choice. This isn't your fault."

"I wanted to help you. I just thought that I could help you, you know? I should've been able to help you."

"You've helped me every single second of every single day, okay? You've helped me more than you could possibly ever know or I could never show you or explain to you, but you are the reason that I have anything good in my life right now."

"It means nothing though, Max. Nothing. You're so sick and nothing else matters but that and there's nothing that I can do to help you."

"It's not your fault, it's on me. It's all on me."

"I just love you so much. I need you to be okay. Can you just be okay? Can you please just be okay?"

"I have to go Cecelia." And she could hear his voice breaking over the words. Small cracks that did more damage to her heart than she was prepared for – and she'd been ready for one hell of an onslaught.

"Max? Please, just two minutes. *Max*. Just one minute." Tears painfully clawed their way from her eyes, so warm they burned as though they were small trails of lava edging down her cheeks.

"I'm sorry. I can't be here right now. I have to go." He was unbuckling his seat belt and swinging open his door.

"I want to know that you're going to be okay. Please just let's calm down for a second before you leave."

But he was already pulling her bags from the trunk and heading towards her apartment building. She followed behind him, trying to steady her breathing.

"I love you, Cecelia, and I completely understand why you have to do this. Okay? I'm not mad; I don't blame you. I know that it's my fault. I just can't breathe right now and I need to go. Can I go? Will you please just let me go?" His voice was edging on desperation and she really didn't want him to go. She knew what his first stop would be.

But that was the whole point of this. She needed to stop worrying about these things and putting him first when she'd been hurting for so long, too. She looked up into his eyes, they were frantic in the moonlight; he looked panicked. She wanted to reach out for him, but it wouldn't do either of them any good. Not now.

"Okay. Yes. Go."

"Okay." And with that he rushed by her and jogged to his car. She was surprised the tires didn't screech from the intensity with which he pulled away.

CHAPTER 18

2015
November

Max was a liar and Cecelia was a fool. These are the things she needed to remember, because they were true, and because they hurt. Everything else must be pushed aside for now, or she was sure that her feet wouldn't move and that her hand wouldn't turn when she gripped the doorknob. Max was a liar; he'd made a fool of her. In this small hour of this big day, Max was not funny or kind or sick or in need of help. He was only a liar, and Cecelia, though a fool she might be, would not stand for a liar in her life.

For the past year, it seemed that she was always trying to remember or trying to forget or trying to remind him or distract him or confuse him. Nothing was straightforward or clear anymore. And, with eyes so glazed and dead, his world was even more blurred than hers.

He loved her, he craved her, three years had not dampened his infatuation with her. But, his body did not shake and turn on itself without her. He didn't feel the slow, clammy descent of torture when she left for a few hours. But his little white pills could do that. So the choice was clear. To him it was love or life and he could live without her.

Cecelia's apartment was dark; she couldn't see a thing. She let her duffle bag fall to the floor at her feet and stood still, waiting for her eyes to adjust to the darkness. She didn't remember picking the bag up off the floor. She didn't remember showering and pulling on her pajamas. She didn't realize her hands were shaking until she finally sat still.

She'd done it. She'd gotten the words out and they were clear. She sat on her bed and reached a trembling hand for the remote control. A distraction. The white noise from the TV became background music; she couldn't pull her eyes away from the sight of her hands in her lap. Gently out of control.

She intertwined her fingers, clasping her palms together and squeezing as hard as she could. She watched as patches of white spread over her knuckles. It made no difference. Still they shook.

She lay down on the bed, resting her head on the pillows, and slid her hands underneath the weight of her thighs. She pushed her legs into the bed, crushing her palms and fingers. Nothing.

Why wouldn't they just stop? She couldn't understand it. How frustrating, to have so little control over her own body.

They were hers, the hands. She should be able to stop them from moving. This shouldn't be happening. She wanted them to just stop. Why wouldn't they just stop? Couldn't she make them understand that this wasn't helping?

She needed help. She needed them to stop. Just stop.

The tears were warm as they crawled down her face, landing cold on the pillow below her.

She needed them to listen. She needed them to stop.

2018
September

As Cecelia had pulled on her silk dress, adjusting it so it hung just right, she began to feel small. She'd been wrong to think that all it would take was a pretty dress and her favorite shade of lipstick to get through this.

ONE TIME, BADLY

It was the difference between lying to strangers and lying to family, or to yourself. She could smile in a conference room and steady her voice and it would work. She could sell that, it was a façade that she could take to the bank on most days, but these weren't strangers she was trying to impress tonight. It was Max. It was only Max.

She thought about how well she still felt that she knew him, about the mannerisms she was sure she'd never forget. She remembered bouncing legs and fidgeting hands and hair that had been pushed back to the point of no return. She would see these things and know his energy was nervous.

Her tells remained the same. She'd told herself all day to avoid chewing her bottom lip and to keep from locking her hands together and ringing them as she spoke. But those were just the signs that she was aware. Who knew what Max might remember, if anything at all.

She gave herself a once over, backing away from the mirror to get as much of her outfit as possible in view. Her dress was sexy without being figure hugging or too short. The shoes gave her legs a long, lean look and her hair was somehow maintaining the subtle wave she'd worked it into last night. She couldn't have asked for more from her own damn self than to pull together this look and have it happen tonight, when she arguably needed it more than ever.

She met herself head on in the mirror, catching her own eye and holding her gaze. There was nothing left to fuss over or to use as a distraction. She'd be leaving in a moment and she just hoped the onslaught of nerves didn't do too much damage.

She could picture herself standing in that mirror now. She'd looked scared, and as the bar grew nearer and everything started to feel more inevitable than ever, she could admit that it was okay to be afraid. It was the most honest emotion coursing through her right now and there was no point in denying it. Fighting down these feelings was just going to make this night even more difficult. She needed to feel her way through it if she was ever going to get to the other side, wherever that might be.

2015
November

The fall into nothingness was supposed to be pleasurably numb. That was the point. Nothing. Not a thing. She wasn't supposed to feel anything. Instead, she felt everything amplified by ten thousand. The emotions were crowded and with no room to breathe they sat stagnant, stubbornly waiting for something to push them around. To either shoo them away or give them a chance to grow. Her mind and her stomach were weighed down with them. She became a zombie, and he became an ache in the pit of her stomach.

The only meal she pretended to eat was lunch and it was only because she didn't want her coworkers getting suspicious. She made sure that there was always a snack on her desk. A container of fresh fruit here, a bag of pretzels there. She'd pick at it every few hours; as if she'd gotten busy and forgotten it was even there.

She made herself a sandwich on white bread every morning, something easy to pull apart. Peanut butter and jelly, mostly. She'd take a bite or two, and slowly, absentmindedly break the rest into smaller pieces as she worked. She'd leave the sandwich in front of her for an hour or so, enough time for it to be noted.

She couldn't put into words the way her mind and her body were feeling. They were on fire; they were nearing implosion at a slowly frantic pace. She could describe it in a million ways, there seemed to be thousands of words for it, but none of them made sense. She was alone in this, as billions of people had been before her.

All she wanted was Max. He was the quick fix here. He was the key to her sanity. She knew that one call to him would set her world straight again. The pain would go away. Even more than that, she would feel happiness. She would feel relief.

She couldn't comprehend how his absence could do this

to her. This had been her choice; she'd had time to mentally prepare for it and everything. Now, she couldn't even remember the girl who'd been strong enough to make any choice at all. She would focus on his arms or his hands or the line of his jaw, as if missing him in pieces would hurt less than feeling the loss of all of him all at once.

And of course there's no accounting for the end in the beginning. It protects itself in this way. She couldn't have known that it would be like *this*.

And someone could tell you exactly how it feels. The sick stomach, the no-eating, no-sleeping bloated feeling of what you're sure is near death. The spinning brain and the pounding memories and the questions and you wouldn't be prepared for it. There simply was no preparing for it.

She stopped listening to music and watching television. Everything became linked to Max. He was every thought in her mind.

Max would love this. Max would hate this. Max needs this. Max would want that.

Everything became something that Max needed to know. Everything became marked by the fact that she didn't know what Max would think about it; that she could never find out for sure.

It was unbearable. It was all she thought about and it was the heaviest thought she'd ever had. He was slowly becoming something more than a person; he was an experience, he was a tragedy that she couldn't make sense of.

And that was another thing. The tears were always there. She cried through her morning routine and all the way to work. She would do her best to turn it all off as she walked into the building. She would train her face to be neutral and, if people thought she was in a bad mood she figured it was better than having them know how messed up she really was. She'd started utilizing her full lunch hour to get some of the pent up tears out so that she could make it through the rest of the day. The tears would be streaming down her face again as soon as she climbed into her car at night.

She swapped her normal wardrobe for things she hadn't worn often, or in ages. She put her favorites aside in favor of these random articles that she'd never worn out to dinner or to the movies. That had never been pulled from her body or warmed by the mere proximity of Max, by the heat of skin reaching towards skin.

This went on for three weeks before her mom showed up with a suitcase in addition to the Tupperware full of soup she'd been forcing Cecelia to at least try to eat at night. When she'd called her mom the day after the break up, she hadn't meant to share each and every terrible detail of what had gone wrong between them, but she did. Conversations with moms were just like that sometimes.

"I didn't know you were going anywhere." She could feel the panic rising in her chest at the thought of being away from her mom, of getting through the day without having her to lean on at night.

"I'm not, Cee. I'm coming to stay with you." She was speaking softly, not to the woman in front of her, but to the child she'd learned to comfort all those years ago.

"Mom, you really don't have to do that. I'm going to be fine, I just need some more time." But her lips were trembling as she said it and, with that, her mom wrapped her up in her arms and held her close.

"I'm doing it as much for me as I am for you. You need me, but I need to know that you're all right. I've been worried sick about you and I think you need a little more help than I've been giving you."

"I'm sorry I'm such a mess all the time. I don't know why I can't handle this. I thought it would be bad for a little bit, but I've been crying for almost a month straight now."

"You're hurting and there's no time limit on that. Especially when you consider what you went through only to have it come to this. You fought so hard and now you just need to get some of that strength back."

"He's all I can think about, I just want to call him. I made the wrong decision. I shouldn't have left. You know? I should have stayed to help him. I'm too weak for this, I can't keep living this way," she was frantic. The words rushed out, tripping over one another in their intent.

"Cecelia you need to breathe. You're going to talk yourself right into a panic attack," her mom was speaking softly, rubbing gentle circles on her back.

"I'm supposed to be stronger than this, though. I'm weak, the weakest person. I can't even stand up on my own two feet."

"These thoughts aren't weakness, sweetie. These thoughts are just you processing the pain. You poor thing, your heart is drowning in sadness. That's not weakness," and the pause in her mother's speech made her eyes travel from the floor to meet her mom's gaze.

"Weakness is following through with these thoughts. You left a dangerous situation, and three weeks and a lot of hurt definitely hasn't made it any better. You are my child, and you are so strong. I've watched it. You had the strength to leave, and that means you have the strength to stay away. Do whatever you need to do to not pick up the phone."

Cecelia realized in that moment that she too was going through withdrawals of her own. From then on his name became something to whisper, or not say at all.

There is a darkness deep enough that it doesn't make you thankful for the light, it makes you forget the light. That's what it was to delete his phone number and take all the pictures down.

Cecelia couldn't shake the feeling that she needed to talk to him again. She never expected the conversation in the car to be the last time they spoke. She needed it not to be. There was so much more to say.

Yes, she'd gotten her point across, but she couldn't possibly have known in that moment that she needed to convey everything she felt for him and always would. She didn't think to tell him about what it meant to her to have to let him go and how she could see her life veering off course now, without him.

She couldn't write. She said a silent prayer every workday that passed without an announcement. If she'd won the spot, if she was in charge of this entirely new venture based solely on the words inspired by her love and fear, how could she tell them that the words were dried up? Her mind was a spinning top; she could barely get a single thought out clearly, let alone construct an article full of them.

It wouldn't make sense. She could see herself sitting down, spewing out some kind of stream of consciousness, verbal doodles intertwining until nothing could be discerned from the twisting lines and darkened sheet.

"Do you want a cup of tea?"

It was Louisiana, home from work an hour late. An hour that had seen Cecelia counting the minutes until she wasn't alone anymore. She hated being by herself, with no chance of distraction, with no one to reassure her that she could get through the few hours that remained in this day.

She'd have to start all over again tomorrow, but that was a concern for the morning. She couldn't stand to look that far ahead without panic rising in her stomach, without squeezing her nails into her palms until they left marks.

It was 7:30 pm. She'd have to wait at least another hour before she could take an Advil PM and drift off to sleep.

"Do you think someone will tell me if Max dies?" she turned towards the kitchen to see Lou preparing two mugs on the counter. "Like will his family call me or will I have to wait until it's on Facebook or something like that?"

"Cee, I thought you deactivated your account," Lou shot her a weary look from across the island.

"I did, but you didn't, did you? You have to keep your eye out for things like this. I doubt his mom is checking on him while he's sleeping. That's when I worried the most."

"Yes, I will tell you if, God forbid, I see something," the kettle whistled and Lou promptly poured the boiling water into the waiting mugs.

She'd chosen an old Harry Potter mug for Cecelia. It was her favorite, adorned with a lightning bolt and glasses, worn from years of use. Cecelia wished she could give Louisiana a smile for the small gesture.

"Thanks, Lou. I know I'm acting crazy. I'm *still* acting crazy, but this is the stuff that keeps me up at night," she settled back on the couch with her steaming cup. Lou took the seat next to her.

"Cecelia, you're allowed to grieve for as long as you want. You're getting yourself to work every day, you're eating at least one meal per day. These are the things we need to focus on. Remember what I told you when this all happened?"

Louisiana never referred to the break up for what it really was. She always just vaguely alluded to it. She might as well have come up with a code name at this point, but there really was nothing else that Cee spoke about so that was probably unnecessary.

"The thing about using WebMD?"

"No, we're past the point of you dying from self-induced starvation, but what a fun memory to reflect on over tea," Lou shot her look to let her know she was joking. "I'm talking about the deserted island thing."

"Sorry, Lou, not ringing a bell."

"Understandable. You looked like a zombie when I was saying it. Scary, really. But you did nod along so I thought maybe I was getting through."

"I'm sorry, I don't remember."

"Okay, so I was explaining to you that when you go through something like this, when you really have your heart broken, time becomes irrelevant and you start to think of what you stand to lose as the zombie that you are as opposed to the human that you were. And you choose maybe three. Three things that you have to have. That you want to be there when zombie you becomes you you. There has to be some life left for you. Make sure of it," she squeezed Cee's hand at this, a silent acknowledgment of the tears running down her best friend's cheeks.

"These things shouldn't relate to your survival, they aren't necessarily the things you'd take to a deserted island, they're the things you'd hope to have waiting for you at home when you're rescued. And, Cee, you're going to be rescued. We're going to help you and you won't feel like this anymore, I promise."

"I can't, Lou. I can't feel like this anymore, it's too much."

"I know, but you're getting better each day, we all see it," this was another vague reference.

Ever since her mom went back home after two weeks at the apartment Louisiana had been in contact with her every day just checking in and giving updates. At first, she'd wondered how her mom just seemed to sense when she was having a particularly bad day, but it was Lou feeding her information. Cecelia couldn't be anything but grateful for the love that was symbolized in those quick notes from her mom to her friend. She hoped someone was monitoring Max as closely.

"I just can't feel anything right now. But I'm trusting you on that one. Better every day, I'll take it."

"I love you, Cee. You're going through hell, but I hope you realize the strength that it's taking for you to choose this path every day. You're fighting for yourself and I admire you so much for it."

"I'm trying, Lou. I know that I have to do this, for me and for him. He needed a wake up call. I just wish that I could check in on him without blurring the lines."

"I know, Cee. But maybe you're better off not knowing for now. It's only been a few weeks. As much time as it's going to take you to start feeling better, Max is in for a longer road. We're just going to focus on you for now, that's all we can do."

"Thanks, Louisiana. I can't say it enough. Thank you."

"You don't have to say it at all. That's what I'm here for."

That night, buoyed by Louisiana's words and the rare moment of clarity that she felt following their conversation, Cecelia began typing a letter. It was all she could think to do with the words that she needed to say. She couldn't see Max, she couldn't call him, because she couldn't guarantee that she'd be able to walk away again.

So she wrote him. She wrote him as if she'd never see him again for as long as she lived. She wrote him as if she'd never post the letter.

Max,

*I believe you to be the love of my life, my soul mate. I thought this before I left and I feel it even more clearly now that we're apart. You are a missing piece of me; you are **the** missing piece of me.*

In leaving, I could never have accounted for an emptiness like this, or for the panic that I feel when I look at my life and you're not in it.

There aren't words for the way it feels to miss you.

The first time I saw you, I think I felt it then. I think I've always known. Now, there doesn't seem to be a me without you. I don't recognize the girl that I've always been and so, I'm changing.

I'll be different the next time you see me, but you'll be different, too. That's the point, that's what I'm wishing for now. That we'll both be different, but enough of the same to be us again.

I know I've killed you in certain ways; I've taken pieces of you and lost my grip on them. What I was hoping to do was to only take the parts that were keeping you stuck. I was trying to force a change in you. If, in my haste, I took other, more important pieces, then I apologize. But I hope you know that I left some of my most important pieces with you as well.

Love,

Cecelia

She would never send it. Instead, she would keep it to give to Max when he was better. She had to hold on to the hope that the day would come when they could be together again and they could make sense of the past year somehow. He would stand before her, cheeks full, eyes lively, and they would put this all behind them once and for all.

From that moment on, Cecelia vowed to take Louisiana's advice. *Find three things in life that you need to keep*; it should've been easy enough. Cee didn't think her family should be considered. She wasn't at risk of losing them. That wasn't the type of family she was from.

She would add her friends to that list, but she realized she didn't really have any of those anymore. Though Louisiana had always been her best friend, Cee always counted a few of the girls from their college years, and even some from high school, as friends. They'd grab dinner or drinks from time to time, which dwindled to a busy group chat complaining about work and money and boys, which all seemed to have disappeared somewhere along the way.

She hadn't considered that she'd been quietly losing pieces of herself all this time. When she really looked at her life, most of the things that she counted as important, that added meaning to her day, had evaporated. She hadn't even noticed them go with the shadow of Max casting a darkness on everything else, shrinking the things around him until they didn't exist anymore.

There wasn't much she could do about it at the moment. She was in survival mode right now; the rebuilding would have to come later. And so her main concern was her job. She'd been scraping by for the past few weeks, but she knew it was only a matter of time before someone noticed that her work wasn't quite cutting it. She couldn't have that happening, not when she was on the brink of really setting herself apart as a writer.

After all, hadn't she wanted a new life? She made a change and she'd learned over time that, even in seemingly unrelated ways, more changes normally followed. It was a cycle of sorts and she was at the start of a new one now. All she had to do was adjust for the curves and try to keep up.

She was lucky to have the boss that she did. Even if he'd noticed that she hadn't quite been herself for the past few weeks, he didn't mention it. And the part that put Cecelia at ease the most was that she hadn't expected him to. He made it clear that life got in the way sometimes and there wasn't much anyone could do about. He wouldn't approach her, but his door was always open should the time come that she felt the need to talk to him.

She'd been tempted to go to him over the past few weeks, but what would she even say? In her mind, Max was really sick and he might even be dying, but she couldn't help. She was only keeping him from getting better, so she'd made the decision to leave. That's how she would like to be able to explain it. But there would need to be more detail, it really made no sense without one important factor and she wasn't willing to share that piece of information with anyone.

She wished she had the freedom to explain herself, to garner some type of understanding from the people around her. She spent every single day with them and it would be so comforting to be able to confide in them, to have them support her through this. But she had a nagging feeling that she'd get more questions than understanding, that she'd put people off by connecting herself to something that was still so taboo. Words like rehab and recovery didn't go over well in a professional setting, as if it were shameful to try and save your own life.

So she was alone and she came to terms with it. She texted Louisiana and her mom throughout the day, just letting them know what was going on. She tried to infuse as much enthusiasm as she could muster into her messages. An exclamation point here, a goofy emoji there. It was so much easier to fake it when they weren't right in front of her.

That was the way ahead, as far as she could tell. Just keep pretending things were fine, until they actually were. She could be her new, sad self around a select few people, but, other than that, she was going to start acting like her old self again. And if she wasn't quite as pleasant or upbeat as she used to be, at least she was trying her best. At least she was trying at all.

The time would come when the happiness and peace that she used to feel would come easily to her. For now, she was going to feel her way through. Her dad had always told her that her sadness was important; it was the best way to understand her strengths and her weaknesses.

Somewhere along the way, Stan had called her in to let her know that the spot was hers. She'd be writing three pieces per day, two curated and one would be the column for the new section. It was still a very tentative position, but it was hers for the taking should the readers respond accordingly. It had hit her as an afterthought before Stan had even gotten the full sentence out. She couldn't even bring herself to feel the tiniest bit of pride.

Now, she was doing her best to focus on her writing, making the decision that a change of tone would have to do because any effort to maintain the voice that she'd had before would be a waste. The one thing that she wanted to avoid at all costs was producing something that rang as false or forced. She'd always written the type of thing that she could relate to, and the column would just have to change with her.

She wrote something up quickly and sent it to Stan, letting him know that it was the start of her next column. She sometimes did this if she wasn't sure about how the topic she was covering would be received, and this was no different. Cee crossed her fingers as she read it through and hit send. She needed his approval; she needed to know that this version of her could still be successful here.

We're sitting at an outdoor table (my request) and splitting a medium rare burger and an order of onion rings (his). The sun is warm, too warm, on my back and there's a bird chirping above us, so loudly it's becoming shrill.

He doesn't hear it, but I do and it's loud enough in my ears to cause distraction. I'm not paying attention to what he's saying, I'm not even sure that he's saying anything at all. Because that's what happens when you realize things aren't working. You start to panic.

Suddenly you're as sensitive as a newborn stepping outside for the first time. Everything is sharp; everything stings. There's a confusion that you can't even begin to grasp.

I start breathing evenly, strong but low, and as quietly as I can manage. I don't need him to see me, because I know him and it hasn't hit him yet that we're not making it work. He's always a little slower to reach these conclusions; I usually drop some hints and let it come to him naturally, if with a few some small nudges.

But no hints this time. None. My lips are sealed on this one, I decide. Maybe he won't ever notice it. Maybe I could unnotice it.

Stan emailed her back an hour later.

Looks good. Darker than usual, but it feels fresh. It's a go.
-Stan

Cecelia smiled at her screen, feeling a bit of confidence return to her. She could do this.

CHAPTER 19

2015
December

"Something's wrong, Lou. It looks totally crooked. Is the stand on tight enough?" Cecelia was crouched down in the middle of her living room, face to face with the wobbliest Christmas tree in town, possibly in the world.

"I don't know. Probably not?" Lou was clearly over decorating. She'd made it a whole twenty minutes before throwing her hands up. "I think I pulled a muscle in my arm on the treadmill last night, I couldn't fasten it as well I wanted to."

"Okay, will you just stand here while I try to fix it? Make sure it's standing up straight, otherwise we'll have to do it again."

With that, Cecelia crawled under the tree, doing her best to close the stand tighter around its stem. It immediately began to fasten, small gaps closing all around. Louisiana must've pulled all of the muscles in her arm if that was the best she could do.

"There! That should be better," Cecelia backed away from the tree and straightened up, giving it a close look. It wasn't perfect, but it didn't look like it would be falling over anytime soon, either.

"Looks great, Cee!" Status update on Lou: still not into it.

"Let's take a break now."

"Sounds good, do you want some hot chocolate? I love drinking hot chocolate in front of the Christmas tree."

"Sure. As long as I can sit my ass on the couch, I'll do whatever you want," Lou's ass was already sat on the couch by the time Cecelia reached the kitchen.

"So I was thinking about something," Cecelia began heating the milk, leaning back against the counter as she spoke.

"Oh yeah? Anything interesting?" Lou twisted around on the couch, meeting Cecelia's eye over the island countertop that separated the rooms.

"I might sign up for a writing class in the city," she didn't know why she was nervous to hear Lou's opinion, but she could feel her cheeks warming a bit as she spoke. "I know I haven't really done it before, but ever since I started the column at work I was thinking that I might want to try creative writing."

"I think it's a great idea, Cee," Lou's enthusiasm was genuine. "That'll be so interesting! Who knows, you could end up writing the next great American novel."

"I wouldn't take it that far just yet, but it's been on my mind lately and it's kind of expensive, but I think the timing is right for something like this," she moved the pot from the heat and poured it into the mugs she'd placed on the counter.

"I'm enjoying the column, but it's kind of easy because I'm usually writing things that have happened to me, or getting stories from my coworkers that they don't mind having published.

"This would be completely different though, more of a challenge. I'd have to make up characters and plotlines myself; everything would be from scratch, which is kind of scary, but I'd have total control."

"That could be so much fun, think of all of the drama you could create," Lou's smile was bright and it made all of the difference for Cecelia. All it took was one vote of support to make a tiny, little dream seem totally realistic.

"Right? I was reading about it and the professors in the

program all seem cool and they had examples on the site of the types of prompts that students get and they all seem so interesting. Obviously, it'll be a bit time consuming, but I think I'm going to really like it."

"I think this is the best idea, Cee," Lou made her way into the kitchen, ripping the hot cocoa packages open and finishing up the job that Cee had started. She handed Cecelia her mug with a small smile, a trace of pride evident on her face. "I'm excited for you."

"Thanks, Lou. I'm excited for me, too." And with that, Cee shot a look at the Christmas tree and took a sip of her hot cocoa, peaceful.

That night, nestled safely in her bed, Cecelia pulled out her credit card and signed herself up for Creative Writing 101, the class she'd been eyeing. A thrill of excitement ran up her spine at the thought of sitting in a room, listening to ideas and watching as the people around her crafted a skill that was so new to her. She couldn't wait for her own thoughts to form a world full of people that she'd dream up.

As Christmas Day rolled around and Cecelia's office began buzzing with talk of booked flights home and packed bags, she took the opportunity to sit down with Stan before he caught his own flight up to Boston to stay with his brother's family for the holidays. It was the first trip home that he'd be bringing his new boyfriend, Greg, and he'd been seriously freaking out over it for the past week.

"How are you doing? Feeling any better about the holidays?" Cecelia asked as she closed his office door behind her and took a seat across from him at his oak desk. At 36 floors up, Stan had a gorgeous view of the city, with buildings spreading out for miles, catching the sun's rays and reflecting them in every direction.

"Not really, but there's nothing I can do. They'll either like him or they won't, it is what it is," he looked resigned as he said it.

She knew that Stan's main concern was the fact that Greg

was a struggling actor. In a family of doctors and lawyers, Stan was already an outcast for choosing to work in publishing. He didn't want to have to deal with his family turning up their noses at Greg simply because he was pursuing a creative career path as well.

"They'll like him. He's too funny not to like. They can try all they want, but he'll have them cracking up in no time," Cecelia had only met Greg a handful of times, but his sense of humor was most definitely the quality that stood out most to her. She often thought that must be what attracted Stan as well, for the entire time she'd known him, he always seemed like he could use a good laugh.

"Hopefully you're right. So as long as you're not here to give me your two weeks notice, I'm just going to stick my chin up and get through it," he was eyeing her carefully. She knew it wasn't every day that she asked to meet with him, but did he really think she'd quit on him the week before Christmas?

"Oh my God, of course not! After all you've just done for me? I'm staying right where I am," she shook her head at the thought.

"Thank God. I just noticed that you haven't been quite yourself lately and that sometimes happens. Someone starts looking for a job elsewhere and they can't even meet your eye anymore."

"Not me. I actually just went through a kind of tough break up, but that's all. I'm really happy here, Stan. I'm not planning on leaving," she blinked back the emotion that threatened to come through. She'd been playing it so cool; she didn't need a single tear rolling down her cheek right now.

"Oh no, not Max! I thought you guys were doing well. I'm so sorry to hear that, Cecelia," he looked genuinely sad at the news. The one thing she'd learned since getting her heart smashed was that it was a completely relatable brand of awfulness. Everyone's been there; it was like joining a shitty club.

"It's okay. I just wasn't feeling like myself for a while, but I'm doing better now," she needed to change the subject.

"What I really came here to talk about though," Stan interjected a quick 'Oh, yes' into her sentence, happy to be getting back on topic. "I signed up for a creative writing class down at Empire Writers and I felt like I should thank you."

"That sounds like a great move! No need to thank me, Cecelia. I'm not the one paying the tuition," Stan joked, clearly more relaxed now that he knew which field they were playing on.

"But it was you who thought that I could start writing like this and I really don't think I would've considered it without you. I'm so excited to start and it all goes back to your encouragement. I just wanted to say how much it means to me to have a boss like you, it makes all the difference."

"You make it easy, Cecelia. There's so much talent and, as your boss I must say, such a fine work ethic. I feel lucky to have you on my team."

"Thanks, Stan, for everything."

"You're so very welcome. Now make sure you're not working too hard before the holiday, we only need two more pieces set to publish before we can take a few days off. It truly is the most wonderful time of the year."

The rest of Cecelia's year was filled with gift shopping and holiday parties. Her coworkers had extended quite a few invitations her way and she happily accepted. She was now the proud owner of three new ugly sweaters, two were for parties that she'd be going to in the city and one was for the small get together that she and Louisiana had decided to throw at their apartment.

She'd asked some of the people she'd been spending time with at work and Lou had invited the clique that she'd slowly grown closer to as well as some of the girls that they'd hung out with in college. Barring any questions from the Rutgers girls about Max, it should be a really fun night.

As the December days passed by and the holidays came and went, Cecelia found herself looking forward to the year ahead. She felt like she'd been trudging through mud for months now and it was finally letting up, turning to solid ground beneath her feet. She had her new writing class to look forward to and she promised herself she'd get back into the gym routine that had been so good for her in college.

Though she hadn't been able to reconnect with any of the girls that she'd lost touch with, she found herself making real friends at work. She'd been saying no to happy hours and nights out for birthdays for so long that she hadn't even considered what she'd been missing. She felt like she was truly at the beginning of something and it was more than she'd been able to imagine just a few weeks before. One change and she'd sparked a whole new movement in her own world.

"Can you pass the broccoli down this way, Cee?" Her dad had already loaded up his plate with chicken cutlet and buttered noodles, so it was only right that he add some greens, if only for the splash of color.

Cecelia lifted the plate of steamed broccoli and handed it over to Sedona to pass to their father. He nodded his thanks as he scooped a spoonful of the vegetable onto his dish.

When her mom had called her that morning asking if Cee wanted to come by for an early dinner she was happy to oblige. Between work, writing class, and her brand new social calendar, she hadn't seen her parents in a few weeks. She couldn't be happier to be seated in their cozy dining room enjoying a home cooked meal. Even Sedona had made the time to join them.

"So the writing class is going well?" her mom finally took a seat at the table. She never could just sit and eat when the food was ready, neurotically loading the dishwasher and wiping the counters down before she joined the rest of the family.

"It is," Cee knew she was being coy, but she was still feeling shy about her new hobby. To her, it was like putting a pipedream on the table for judgment. "It's only been a few weeks, but the instructor is really helpful and everyone there is so smart. I didn't realize how much I missed school until now."

"Working on anything interesting?" her dad had taken up his own line of questioning. "I would love to read anything you've written and I know your mom would, too."

Her mother eagerly nodded her approval as finished chewing her bite, "Oh, Cee, we really would love it."

"I don't really have anything ready yet. We're still just getting into structure and that sort of thing, but we have a final project and you guys can definitely read that," she said it with more certainty than she felt.

Part of the appeal of this class was that no one knew her there. She felt a freedom in that and she didn't want the pressure of a familiar audience to affect whatever she decided to write about.

"Guys, there's no way Cee goes on this free woman adventure and starts following her dreams in New York City and writes something appropriate for her mom and dad to read over the morning coffee," Sedona took this opportunity to pipe up, nearly reading Cecelia's mind exactly. She loved when that happened. "But she'll let me read it and I'll let you guys know if she's any good."

"Did you hear that, Laurie?" her dad couldn't help but smile at his youngest. "Sedona is going to relay the message. That means we've got at least six months in between the time when Cecelia finishes class and Dona slows down long enough to speak to us to guess at what Cee wrote. We should make it a game; bet on subjects and word count. Could be fun, no?"

"Dad!" Sedona broke through her parent's laughter. "I'm here every single day! I don't know why you guys are always making me seem like an absentee daughter."

"You're here every day because you live here, honey. That doesn't mean you talk to us every day. Ask your mom; we have a chart somewhere from over the summer. I think we were going on seventeen days of silence at one point."

"There's no way that's true! Unless it was when I was dating that guy who worked at the pier. Then maybe your chart stands," Sedona shrugged, used to her parents ragging on her. She really was the busiest person Cee had ever met.

Cecelia couldn't help but join in her parent's laughter,

despite the dirty look Sedona shot her.

"I'm keeping my mouth shut on this one!" which was really just a way for her mom to agree with her dad. The look on her face was proof enough. Cecelia was sure that somewhere along the line her mom would be taking that bet.

"Donie, how are your classes going?" Sedona was in her sophomore year at William Paterson, where she was a standout member of the soccer team.

"My classes are going terribly as always," Sedona forked a piece of chicken and looked up at Cecelia before taking a bite. "I don't understand your stance on school at all, it really and truly sucks. You're such a freak for going back, even if it's just for one class."

"You know, I don't know why I don't come over here for dinner more often," Cecelia took a healthy sip of red wine as her parents burst out laughing.

CHAPTER 20

2016
April

Louisiana was already snuggled up on the couch, glass of white wine in hand, catching up on Grey's Anatomy when Cecelia got home. Cee glanced at the TV.

"Oooh this episode is so good," she plopped down on the couch and stole some of Lou's blanket.

"Don't say a word!" Lou didn't even bother to look over at Cecelia as she said it.

"Okay, crazy. I'm not you, I don't ruin shows for no reason," that earned her a sharp glance.

She held her hands up in innocence and trained her eyes on the screen. She really did love this episode. She was just about to head to the kitchen to see if she could find a bottle of red to uncork when she heard her phone buzzing from its spot on the coffee table, the screen lighting up with a name she wasn't sure she'd ever see again.

Her heart skipped a beat, then stopped.

Elaine Maylor

"No," she could feel the tears stinging at her eyes already. She could only think of one reason for Mrs. Maylor to be calling her at 8:30 pm on a Sunday night.

"Cee?" Louisiana quickly paused the TV, leaving just the sound of Cecelia's iPhone vibrating against the glass table in the room. "Cee, you have to answer that. She wouldn't be calling you if she didn't have a good reason to."

Cecelia could tell that Louisiana was scared, too.

"I can't. I can't answer it. Please don't make me," she was panicking now, suddenly sobbing. "I don't want to know, Lou. I don't want to know."

"Wait, just wait, Cecelia," Lou's hand was on Cecelia's arm, steadying her. She reached for the phone. "Let's see if she leaves a voicemail. If it's that bad, she would never leave it on your voicemail. She'll just wait for you to call her back."

They both stared intently at the phone as it ceased ringing. Waiting, waiting. Then it buzzed again, signaling that a voicemail had been left.

"Play it on speaker, Lou," Cecelia wiped at her eyes.

"Okay. I'm here, okay? Right here next to you no matter what," Louisiana navigated her way to the voicemail box on Cecelia's phone, finding the message that had just come in. She hit play.

Max's mom sounded awful. Her voice was quiet, strained. She sounded like a lost little girl, rather than the vibrant woman that Cecelia had know her to be.

"Hi, Cecelia. I'm so sorry to be bothering you, especially this late at night, but I was hoping to catch you at home. I'm having a bit of trouble with Max," she paused for a moment as her voice broke, "and I was hoping to talk to you for a few minutes. I know that this isn't a part of your life anymore and I've pushed off this phone call for quite some time hoping I wouldn't have to make it, but if you have some time this week maybe we could get coffee? Max won't know about any of this, I just have a few questions and I'm hoping you can help me. And, sweetie, I totally understand if you say no, I just had to try. For Max. Thanks, Cecelia."

Lou gently placed the phone back on the table and turned to Cecelia, letting out a quiet breath.

"Thank God. He's okay, Cee," she sounded hopeful, "it's all okay."

"He's alive, but I doubt he's okay. She sounded terrible, that poor woman," Cecelia wiped at her eyes again, trying to steady her breathing. She needed to calm down.

"He's putting her through hell, that's for sure," Lou shook her head. She never quite had the sympathy for Max that Cee had hoped she would.

"I guess I'm not surprised, but somewhere in my head I've been imagining him all better," she knew it was stupid and almost wished she hadn't said it out loud, but this was still just so hard to wrap her head around.

"You're not going to meet up with her are you? I mean I know you'd like to help out, but that's the whole reason you ended it. There's nothing else that you can do, Cee," Lou was already trying to convince her against a decision she'd yet to even make.

"Lou, can I just process this for like a half a minute before you jump down my throat about it?" Cecelia didn't mean to sound so harsh, but the last thing she needed was Lou getting mad at her for this.

It was her decision and she needed to live with it. But Lou had to live with her, so she could see why she might feel strongly about Cecelia avoiding the possible ramifications of a conversation like the one she was bound to have with Mrs. Maylor. Especially when she'd just starting to get herself together again.

"I'm sorry, I just think you should think about. Sleep on it, okay? Don't respond to her tonight, not when you're all worked up," her voice was even, but Cee could hear the plea in it.

"I won't answer tonight. I don't even know what to say. Obviously, if she's reaching out she thinks I can help somehow and I want to be able to do that, but I'm not going to set myself up for another fall. I'll think about it, Lou. I promise," she leaned over and hugged her friend. "I'm going to take a shower and get some sleep. Finish the rest of this episode, the last like two minutes are completely nuts."

"Okay, night, Cee. Love you," she looked worried and Cee hated that. In just five minutes, she'd ruined Louisiana's peaceful Sunday night.

"Love you too, Lou."

Cecelia's whole body felt exhausted as she walked back to her bedroom, as if those few moments had taken everything out of her. She hadn't felt real fear like that in a while; she was guessing that's what really did her in. Panic was wearisome, even in small doses.

She sat on her bed for a minute, pulling at a loose thread in her comforter and staring at her phone. She was tempted to play the voicemail again, but what good would that do? Just one listen and she already had Elaine Maylor's broken voice on repeat in her mind. *For Max*, she had said.

Cecelia grabbed her slippers and robe and made her way to the bathroom for a long, hot shower. She was planning on thinking it over in the calm of the warm water, but she already knew what her decision would be.

For Max.

She texted Mrs. Maylor during her lunch break the next day. She hadn't discussed it with anyone, hadn't even told her mom about the voicemail, but she didn't want to be talked out of it. Logically, she knew this wasn't the best idea but, as she'd told Lou, she had to live with her decision.

Cecelia Scott met with Elaine Maylor because she felt in her stomach that it was the right thing to do. Cecelia Scott met with Elaine Maylor because she needed to speak with his mother. She wanted to make sure that someone was taking care of him, someone with the ability to put him back together. Cecelia Scott met with Elaine Maylor on Wednesday night at 7 pm. She wasn't a second late.

They chose Starbucks because everyone goes to Starbucks for meetings like this. The kind of meeting where you don't want to question the setting, the tone, the drink that will grow cold in front of you as you struggle to bring words to your mind, as you push them from your mouth hoping that they sound right.

She looked into Max's eyes as his mother grew more

desperate with each passing moment. She wasn't asking Cecelia to come back; she would never do that. She praised her for having the nerve to leave, to make a hard decision when one needed to be made. What Max's mother wanted was answers; she needed advice. She was his mother, yes, but Cecelia had belonged to him. She knew more, she had to. Someone had to know more.

They'd hugged when they'd seen each other, Cecelia taking comfort in the fact that, although she had sounded awful in the voicemail that she'd left, Elaine looked good. Her hair was styled in it's usual 'do, falling straight to her shoulders with a curve at its tips. She was wearing a green sweater and dark jeans, a pair of knockoff Uggs on her feet. Max's family lived comfortably, but his mother wasn't the type of woman to spring for a real pair.

Cecelia had made sure to wear something comfortable to work, so that she wouldn't be bothered wearing it for a few hours longer. She was grateful that wide leg pants had come back in style. She'd matched her favorite pair with a tight white turtleneck and black heels. Sophisticated, yet comfortable. There was no better way to go.

On the bus home, she'd pulled her long chestnut waves into a neat bun and applied a coat of rosy lipstain. She wanted to look presentable. She wanted the past few months of hell to have no place in her appearance. She truly didn't think that Mrs. Maylor would go back on her word and tell Max that they'd met, but Cee wanted the woman to know that she was doing fine. She couldn't put her finger on the reason, but it felt important to her. It had all day.

"Cecelia," Mrs. Maylor said her name as they'd hugged, the motherly affection still there despite the circumstances in which they now found themselves. "Thank you so much for agreeing to meet with me. I know it probably wasn't an easy decision, but I truly appreciate it."

Cecelia sat down at the small table that Elaine had found for them. Though there wasn't a great deal of privacy in the café, they were tucked back in a corner, away from most of the other patrons.

"Of course, Mrs. Maylor," Cecelia found herself emotional as she spoke to Max's mom. She'd probably seen him that morning; she talked to him every day. It was the connection to him that Cecelia had been longing for. "I know that it might not seem like it, but all I want is for Max to be okay. To get better."

"I know you do. Don't think for a second that Max's father or I judge you for the decision you made. Most days, I wish that I could get away from this mess, too. I'm ashamed to even say it, but it's not something I would wish on my worst enemy. Watching Max go through this, I didn't know something could weigh this heavily on my heart. It's unbearable pain, as you know."

"I know. I'm so sorry that you guys are going through it," Cecelia paused. "I thought maybe I could give him a wakeup call, but I'm guessing that hasn't been the case."

Mrs. Maylor let out a sad little laugh at that, "It doesn't seem to be going that way. Max is angry, Cecelia. It's probably a side of him you didn't really get to see too much of, but he's been cruel lately. He's not the boy I raised, that's for sure."

"I think I got a little taste of that, towards the end. It's part of the reason I started having doubts in the first place. It's how he eventually came to tell me what was wrong."

Elaine nodded in understanding, "That was actually one of the questions I wanted to ask you tonight. I know that it's probably painful for you, but I was hoping to just get some insight on how you and Max came to an understanding.

He mentioned that you were trying to help him this past year and that you'd even gone through withdrawals with him. Would you be open to talking about what happened with me?

I'm trying to get a better idea of what he's been through and where he stands. Of what may have worked in the past and of what didn't. I'm going to be taking a medical leave from work starting at the end of the month and I'm just trying to lay some groundwork for myself. My son needs help, Cecelia and I'm going to get it for him."

Cecelia blinked back tears at that, fear and relief flooding her. Max had to be in bad shape for Elaine to put her life on hold, but she was so grateful to know that some type of action was being taken on Max's behalf.

She tried not to picture him as he would look now. Angry and thin, cheek bones cutting hard across his face, skin dull, eyes tired. She didn't want to see it, was grateful that he still seemed himself on that last weekend. She tried to remember him on that first night, leading her through that crowded frat house, smiling, telling her he'd be looking for her. She wondered how Mrs. Maylor preferred to remember him, or if it was too painful to think of chubby cheeks and knobby knees at this point in their story.

"Thank you, Mrs. Maylor. Thank you for doing this. He needs help," Cecelia couldn't keep her voice from shaking. "He's been really needing help."

"Thank *you*, Cecelia. For all that you did for him and all that you tried to do. I know it must've been one hell of a spot to be in, but you may have kept him alive just a little bit longer and I'll always, always be grateful to you for that."

Cecelia shook her head at that, her stomach sinking, "I don't know. I've been thinking that I should've called you or just taken him to rehab. I wasn't really thinking clearly and I was letting him make all of the decisions. I don't think I did the right thing."

"Oh, Cecelia," Elaine reached across the table and grabbed Cecelia's hands in her own, holding them tightly. "Don't ever feel bad about how you handled a situation that was completely out of your hands. Max should never have put this on you, he was wrong to ask you for that kind of help."

Max's mom seemed to struggle with her own thoughts for a moment, before meeting Cecelia's eyes again, releasing her hands and retreating back to her own side of the table.

"Can I say something?" at Cecelia's nod, Elaine continued. "I don't think I can put into words what it feels like to go through this, but you'd know better than anyone else would."

She paused, clearing her throat.

"Since the moment Max was born, I've been so grateful for his health. It's a parent's worst nightmare to have a sick child and he was my first baby. I had no idea what it would be like and I hadn't even considered half of the things that could go wrong. In the hospital, when they were checking his eyes and his ears I felt this panic. I hadn't considered all of the basic things that might be wrong with him, that would make his life so much more difficult. But he was fine, I took him home and he was so bright and happy and healthy. I just felt like it was such a gift and we were so lucky to have this perfect little boy.

And every year he got older, he grew stronger and stronger. He barely even had colds as a kid. I felt like I had Isabella at the doctor's office every other week, but Max was never like that. I thank God all the time for giving me such a strong and capable child. We've watched him learn to walk and run and play sports and be so, so powerful. I know it sounds simple, but when you have a child you can't imagine all of the small victories that they'll have. Watching him run the ball and score and beat out other players, you just can't really picture how proud you'll be of your kid for things like that.

He was always so strong, Cecelia. And this? This is such a slap in the face. His health is one of the miracles of my life, and he's just letting it slip away. And when I tell him this, he doesn't even hear me. He's taking everything for granted and it makes me sick."

Elaine looked shaken by her own words, as if she hadn't meant to say all that, but at some point the words had come on their own. Cecelia was sure she'd never said them out loud before and she felt in that moment that she truly understood why Mrs. Maylor had called her.

She had gotten out. She'd been in the very same mess and she'd simply walked away from it. She felt bad now, for her sophisticated clothes and her fresh coat of lipstick. Cecelia didn't know what to say.

"I'm sorry. I think I went a bit too far. Just seeing you

sitting here after your day of work in the city, I'm proud of you Cecelia. I know that you don't need me to say it, but you're doing so well for yourself and it's another precious thing that Max has cost himself. I think of his future and I used to be so excited to see all of the things he would do and now it just hurts."

"I'm so sorry, Mrs. Maylor. I know that feeling, to be so lost in everything that's happening that you can't even see past it. To be scared that there isn't anything past it.

When Max and I broke up, it was awful. I felt like my heart had been ripped out of my body and there was just like this painful, gaping hole in my chest that wouldn't ever heal. I couldn't eat or sleep or think straight, I really thought I might die from it. But it was still better than watching him kill himself.

No matter how bad I was feeling, I knew that I made the right choice because nothing I had done had helped him. And if I couldn't help him, I at least wanted to be able to remember our relationship for the amazing thing that it was. I left before it could get worse and it was selfish, but he was so good to me right at the end that I can never regret doing that for myself, and for the pieces of him that I wanted to always remember."

"It makes me so happy to hear that. He came home from that trip so lost. He was in his room for days and I was worried that maybe he'd lost control and done something to you. That's part of the reason that I've been so reluctant to call you. But now I need to know, anything that you can share with me is helpful."

Cecelia nodded, trying to pool together any victorious moments that they'd had, any conversation that had gone the right way. She told Mrs. Maylor anything she could think of, watched as Max's mom absorbed that information, a determined look in her eyes. It was as if Cecelia was sending her on a secret mission, giving her the codes and instructions that would get her through to the end.

As she looked into his mother's eyes, she so wanted to see Max again. Just for a second. She wanted to look out the rain-streaked café window and see him standing just outside, peering in at her. She would walk across the room and swing open the door, embracing the chill in the air, and wrap her arms around him. She would press her face to his chest and just breathe.

2018
September

That meeting with Elaine Maylor had been the last time she'd ever had a conversation about Max that didn't involve tears over missing him, or cursing him for making it so damn hard for her to find someone new, someone who could compare. Until a few months ago, when Joe reconnected with Max, it had been the last time she knew how he was doing.

She'd spent a lot of time thinking about Elaine after that, imagining her hovering a hand over Max's face while he slept, waiting to feel his breath hit her palm. She pictured her grabbing his head in her hands, begging him to meet her eyes and come back from wherever it was that had taken such a hold of him. She could see her sitting alone in her cozy living room, devastated and scared, praying for her miracle to come back to her.

She tried only to think of Max when it was absolutely unavoidable. That meant keeping him out of daydreams and random thoughts. If she came across something that triggered a memory, well there wasn't much she could do about that. But the days of her walking past a store and thinking Max would love that, or hearing a song and wanting to play it for him, those days were gone. She needed to do this favor for herself.

As she moved along in her life, meeting new people and experiencing new things, she didn't mention Max. About a year ago, she'd gotten into a conversation with a few coworkers turned friends at a happy hour downtown. She'd hopped the 2 train and headed to the Financial District with a few of the girls from the office. They'd been talking about it for weeks, FiDi Friday they were calling it.

The idea was to put themselves in a position to meet

men from a different area in the city. They'd all agreed that the Financial District would be a good place to start. The chances of marrying rich were high there, which was something they'd laughed about since making the plan. Hey, if you had to pick someone to spend your life with you might as well pick someone who could give you a good one.

Cecelia wasn't quite sold on the whole finance guy thing, they're reputation as a whole wasn't great. Douche was the word that could often be used to describe your average Wall Streeter, that or Finance Bro. Neither seemed to be something that she was looking for, but 'what she was looking for' hadn't made in appearance in nearly two years, so she was willing to mix it up, if only for a night.

She and the three girls she'd gone with had ended up getting horribly drunk and while she did exchange numbers with someone, she could barely remember what he looked like the next day and couldn't bring herself to answer they 'Hey cutie' text that he'd sent a few days later.

What she did remember was the conversation they'd had on the train downtown. They'd all had a glass or two of wine at the office as they'd wrapped up their day, something that was a normal occurrence throughout the office to ring in the weekend. Their respective buzzes had them feeling chatty and emotional on their ride downtown, when Lita, one of the girls that worked a few rows away from Cee and had become one of her closest work friends, brought up failed relationships.

"It just sucks, you know, that we have to go all this way to try and find someone to date us. We're catches, it shouldn't be this much work," Lita may have had more than two glasses of wine, but no one was going to hold it against her.

"I second that," that comment came from Brynn, she wasn't in Cee's department so she wasn't as close with her as the other girls, but she always enjoyed her company.

"Third," Cee jumped in.

"Honestly, I already know what's going to happen," Nora, Cee's best work friend, added. "I'm going to get too drunk to meet anyone and text Liam the second we leave the bar."

Liam was Nora's ex and she couldn't seem to stop going back to him, not that Cee could blame her. The boy was gorgeous and always made himself available to Nora. Though her friend had told her that the breakup was mutual, she had a feeling that it was more Nora's idea than Liam's.

"Maybe you should just get back with him, Nor. You clearly still have a thing for him," said Lita, hanging desperately onto the bar in front of her despite the fact that the train was currently stalled.

"I can't! We broke up for a reason and I don't want to just forget about that because I'm bored or lonely or whatever it may be on a given day. I don't love him and I have to stop pretending that I do," Cecelia gave Nora credit for that. She had said that she just couldn't see herself being with Liam long-term and she didn't see a point in wasting any more time with him.

"Ugh don't even mention the L word or you'll have me calling approximately three men who definitely do not want to be hearing from me tonight," Brynn shuddered. "Sometimes the drinks just hit me wrong and I honestly believe I'm still madly in love with these losers I never should've dated in the first place."

"Hear, hear!" Nora seemed happy that someone there might be able to dissuade her from sending the Liam text later tonight.

"What about you, Cecelia? Ever been in love?" Brynn had no idea about Max. Nora was the only one who even knew he existed and, as far as she knew, he was just Cee's college boyfriend, none of the gory details.

Cecelia took a second before she answered, willing the wine in her system to lay low. She didn't need to be spilling her soul in this dirty subway car. So she simply nodded her head and allowed for a small smile.

"One time, badly."

Though her conversation with Elaine stayed with her, Cecelia had allowed it to give her the bit of closure that she'd been searching for since Max sped from her doorway, leaving her standing there with her bags at her feet. He wasn't well, but he was being cared for. Whenever she got stuck on him, or she felt her heart randomly begin to race as she sorted through work emails or sat down to eat dinner, she reminded herself that he was being cared for.

And though the sadness was mostly gone, it floated around the edges of her - just faintly present. It was in her fingers and toes, not holding her back anymore, but weighing her down just that little bit. She'd accepted that it might always be there.

She'd tried purging herself of it. Tried everything she could think of to finally let go of all of the ways that her sadness over Max still affected her life, but nothing made it go away. It wasn't until she'd spent so long not talking about him, that she realized maybe she'd gone about it the wrong way.

She could do something for herself, something quiet and personal that might finally allow her to find peace with the guilt and the devastation that still kept her from sleep, even three years later.

Cecelia decided to do the thing she'd avoided doing. She would write it all down. She would change their names and some of their story, but she would finally allow herself to get it all out without fear of judgment or shame.

It does take time and everybody says that, but no one ever explains why it takes so damn long. Longer than it makes sense for it to take. It's because you're bound to him by a million moments that exist in the back of your mind that you aren't even aware of. You don't even consciously think of these memories but you can see them and they still give you comfort.

So, she would give them 80,000 words on Max. And though she was no longer quite the Cecelia that she had been, and Max was fading slowly into a part of her mind that didn't allow for much more than a short visit, she would sign it with her name. And she would call him all that he was. Because trouble, and sadness, and despair are only bad if you make nothing of them. And because we reject them outright, and because those around us work so that we're able to let them go, these dark emotions are more fleeting than joy.

She would find a way to explain all that he had meant to her and all that she still felt that she was losing. She wouldn't tell her friends that she was still missing the milestones that she and Max would never hit, but she could give those feelings to the girl that she would create.

Let her miss Max and let Cecelia finally move on from him. Because what are we except a compilation of our memories and how they made us feel. We are a fine-tuned reaction to everything we've ever seen or done or had done to us.

And maybe this girl could have one more conversation with Max. Maybe *she* would get to say the things that had made a permanent residence on the tip of Cecelia's tongue should the chance ever present itself for her to say them. She would take her time and get it right. She would close this chapter of her life by opening a new one.

Cecelia didn't tell anyone she was considering writing a book, she looked at it as a side project and worked on it sporadically. She didn't give herself a deadline and she allowed herself the time it took to reflect on all of the feelings that she unearthed in the process.

Was life easier without him? The obvious answer was yes, but it wasn't exactly true. Loneliness can be just as hard, sometimes even more so, as the work it took to be with him.

For now, she was successfully alone. It was more through circumstance than choice that she found herself still single years after her breakup with Max, but she saw no point in pursuing the men that she'd gone on dates with, not when they didn't ignite a spark even close to the one that Max had lit on the night they'd first met.

Cecelia tried to tell herself that things were different now, that *she* was different now. She wasn't going to meet a guy and fall into the charm trap that a 20-year-old version of herself was susceptible to. She needed to give it more of a chance. No amount of convincing could get her to warm to them, so she went with her gut. She was confident that she'd find someone eventually, but she couldn't bring herself to force it. It would come when she was ready and she was hoping that the purging she was doing through her writing would do the trick.

She was not wallowing in her sadness and there was a certain amount of pride to be taken in wanting someone, but never crossing the line into needing to have someone. That was dangerous territory and she was happy to be closed to the option of dating all of the wrong people just to ease the worried voice in the back of her mind that was associating being single with shame.

She would write of Max's quick smile and wrinkled t-shirts. She would write of his shaking hands and pale face. She would write of her own despair and the sickness that had stayed with her for months. She would explain how it wasn't until all of the good things in her life started crawling back to her, that she was sure she'd done the right thing.

The further away she got from the relationship, the more she wondered about him. At the time when everything was happening, she was so focused on how she was feeling and how she would recover that she didn't consider him. She knew, without a doubt, that she was still on his mind. It would be impossible for him to not think about her.

But as time passed she wondered more and more what he was doing. She thought less about her own feelings on everything and more about his. The more probable it became that he was in fact not thinking about her, the more she couldn't help but think about him.

She thought of her own mind and its tendency to recall him, even after all this time. For a while, she viewed this as an acute weakness, an inability to let go and move on. But now, many changes and a few years later, she appreciated the memory of him.

It was a nice reminder of how real she could be, of the depth within herself that she was open enough to expose. It took bravery and true selflessness to share what she and Max had. Instead of thinking of it as weakness, it was a reminder of great strength. And it gave her hope that she would be able to do it all again.

CHAPTER 21

2018
September

Cecelia let out a sharp curse as her mascara wand slipped sloppily across her eyelid, leaving a trail of dark black liquid behind. She'd dreamt of him again, reigniting a low-grade, half-remembered heart sickness that she thought she'd left behind. And, even watered-down, that kind of pain still hurt like hell. This was all the power Max had left and she was thankful for it, but it was still something she couldn't ignore.

She could hear Louisiana fumbling around in the kitchen, probably nursing the same hangover that had Cee's tired eyes doing their best to correct the mess she'd made on her face. Today would be Louisiana's last day in their shared apartment before she moved in with Joe.

They'd decided to spend their last night as roommates toasting to the good times, of which there were apparently five bottles of wine worth. Louisiana had taken a half day at work in order to meet the moving van out front at 2 pm. Cee was in for a full day of torture.

She'd debated taking the day off, but she knew she would just sit around feeling sorry for herself. She was genuinely happy for Louisiana and the step she was taking, but that didn't mean she was ready to say goodbye to the best roommate she'd ever had just yet.

"Cecelia!" Lou was yelling from the kitchen. Where she'd found the strength to even speak at the moment, Cee had no idea. "Juice!"

Now that quick throwback had Cecelia scrapping the attempt of makeup all together. She was bound to cry it off anyway if Lou insisted on walking down memory lane today.

"Yeah?" Cee walked into the kitchen, noting that she had 25 minutes before she needed to head to the bus.

"Do you remember the first night in the dorm room? When we tried to play twenty questions to learn more about one another and only made it like three rounds before we were talking like we'd always known each other?"

"I really don't want to do this Lou," Cecelia remembered the night well. She was so happy to have found a friend so quickly in her new world.

"I know, I know. I just feel so mushy today. It's the end of an era," Cee could see the tears pooling in Lou's eyes.

"Come on, Lou. If you cry I'm going to cry and it took all I had in me today to get this mascara on my lashes."

"I'm just scared, I think. What if Joe and I make it to round twenty of twenty questions? What if we move in together and realize we can't stand one another?"

"That's definitely not going to happen. You guys are meant to be; you know that. You spent two years pining after him and trying to forget him with absolutely no success. That should be all the proof you need."

"I know, you're right. I just feel so weird," Lou shook her head, as if trying to knock the feeling away.

"It's just a change, you'll adjust in no time. I'm sure Joe is feeling the same way, but I know how excited you are about this. He's your fiancé, this is the next step."

"It's just that I was so surprised when he proposed. I was happy obviously, I love him and I want to be with him, but now everything is changing and I just think I'm still trying to adjust to the fact that I have a wedding to plan and now I'm moving to a whole new place and it's just a lot."

"It's just nerves! You'll be twenty minutes away, I can come over whenever you want and you can come hang here anytime, too. You're going to love living with him, I know it."

"And you're going to be okay by yourself?" the tears were back in Lou's eyes as she looked at Cee. "I'm not abandoning you here?"

"Lou, are you serious?" Cee stood up and reached for Lou, giving her friend a hug as she spoke. "I'm so happy for you. If anything, all of these amazing things that you have going on are just making me excited for what's to come for me too. I promise."

"I just know that Max is going to be around again. Joe seems to be with him more and more. I'm starting to get nervous that he's going to try and put him in the wedding party."

"Lou, I'm totally fine. If Max is around, Max is around. It's been almost three years, I've come a long way since I let Max Maylor ruin my day."

"I know, I just feel like a bad friend. Like I'm leaving you when you're going to need me the most."

"You're not leaving me! You're moving three towns away. You better believe I'll be on your doorstep the second I need you."

"Do you promise?"

"Yes, I promise."

That weekend, after she'd moved back into a one bedroom that was nearly identical to the place she'd had before Louisiana's promotion, Cee remembered the peace that came with having her own place.

She played music throughout the apartment as she made breakfast without a care for someone sleeping in the next room. She lit her favorite scented candles, even the ones that had given Lou a headache. She cried a bit without having to worry that Lou would come rushing in to help her.

She wrote in the living room and left her laptop open on the coffee table without the fear that Lou would come across the work she was doing. She felt like a real adult for the first time in years and the independence was incredible.

It had taken her awhile to understand it and to embrace it, but she'd built a life she could really be proud of and the reward was this inner peace that she was able to carry with her even on her bad days. She knew herself, she knew how to protect herself and how to propel herself forward and it was such a gift.

She bought a few new pieces of furniture to differentiate this apartment from her last one and she invited her friends over for wine on Saturday night without checking to make sure Lou was okay with it. There were certainly aspects of having a roommate that she missed, but for right now she was enjoying being on her own.

She was in a position at work where money wasn't an issue for her, having moved into an editorial role with six writers under her. The section had been a success and her column was still well received even three years on. So she spent the first few weeks post-Louisiana treating herself.

She went to the spa, she ordered takeout every night, and she bought nearly an entirely new wardrobe. The only food that had been cooked in her new place was prepared by her mom when her family had come to visit for the first time. She knew it was only a matter of time before she reverted back to her more conservative routine, but for now there was no one to tell her to rein it in.

She'd just gotten a fresh haircut, something shorter and more trendy than she'd ever had before, hitting her just above her shoulders and bouncing with a volume that her longer cut never would've been able to pull off, when she met her mom for lunch in town.

"Well, don't you look gorgeous! I didn't know you were getting a haircut," her mom beamed at her as she sat down in the seat across from her.

"I was just going for a trim, but I figured why not change it up," Cee dragged a hand through her locks, noting the quickness with which she ran out of hair to run through. "You like it?"

"I love it! It really suits you, sweetie. Shows off that beautiful face," her mother's face changed, taking on a more thoughtful look than the moment before. "You really are a grown up, huh?"

"I think so, Mom," Cee laughed. "I've been trying to act like one lately. At least someone noticed."

"You just look so mature, sitting there with your sophisticated haircut. It's like you're glowing with it."

"I've been feeling really different over the past few weeks. Ever since I was back on my own, it's like something in me changed. I can't really explain it, but I'm happy."

"That's so good to hear, Cee," her mom squeezed her hand across the table. "You have no idea how glad I am to hear that."

"Mom?" Cee questioned. "Is everything okay?"

"Oh, yeah. Just with Sedona moving out, I'm feeling like my kids really aren't kids anymore. Now I'm just stuck in the house with your father," Laurie laughed.

"Your kids will always be your kids, Mom," Cee shot her mom a look across the table. "Especially Sedona, that girl is never going to grow up."

"You got that right," they shared a laugh as the waiter came to take their order: two cups of French onion soup and two house salads.

"So what's new with you? Work's still good?" Laurie squeezed her lemon slice and dropped it into her water glass.

"Yup, still loving it. I'm finally feeling like I have a handle on the new writers and I think the section is looking really good. Stan seems happy so something is going right," Cee took a sip of her own water.

"That's great. And the new apartment is all right? You're not feeling too lonely? I worry about you being there all by yourself."

"There are hundreds of other residents in the building, Mom. I'm hardly all by myself. And I really am loving living alone. I just feel free for right now and, if I'm feeling lonely I just have people over or stop by you guys and I'm all good."

"If you're sure. You know there's always a room for you at home if you ever feel like spending the night."

ONE TIME, BADLY

"I know, Mom. Maybe I'll come by next weekend and we can watch a movie?"

Her mother's eyes lit up at that and she launched into a list of the new movies that were on demand that she'd been wanting to see. Right then, Cecelia promised herself to spend more time with her mom, rather than just shooting a text or making a quick call when she had a second. She may be an adult, but she still had a mother who loved to see her.

Cecelia was lowering the heat on a pot of sauce later that night when she heard her phone begin to buzz on the countertop beside her. She'd gotten sick of takeout a few weeks back, after her initial period of independence had worn off. She found herself getting really into cooking her own meals and was even giving her mom's gravy recipe a try tonight.

Lou's name flashed across the screen and Cee inwardly groaned. Louisiana had officially begun wedding planning and, though she hadn't made anything official, it seemed that the maid of honor duties were falling squarely on Cee's shoulders. She'd already dealt with three meltdowns this week and she was praying that this wasn't another one. There was only so much she could say when it came to venue prices and dress shops that weren't open when it was convenient for her friend.

Cee wiped her hands on a towel and swiped across her phone, watching as the call connected, before putting Lou on speakerphone. She began chopping up some lettuce for a small salad as she spoke.

"Hey, Lou. What's up?" She kept her voice bright in the hopes that Lou would think before jumping into a rant.

"Not much, what are you up to?" she sounded fine, thank goodness.

"Just cooking dinner. Everything all right?" Cee threw her freshly chopped lettuce into a colander and gave it a good rinse.

"Oh yeah, everything's good. Everything good with you?"

"Lou, you're being weird. What's going on?" Cee grabbed the phone and took it off of speaker mode. "Did something happen?"

"No, no! Everything's good. I just wanted to invite you to come get drinks on Thursday night," from the tone of Lou's voice, it sounded more like she was inviting Cee to a funeral.

"Okay, yeah sure. Drinks for anything specific?"

She was trying to tip toe around, as Lou had been doing, but she was already getting nervous.

"Well, Joe and I are trying to get everyone together for a little engagement celebration and you're obviously my maid of honor so I want to make sure you're free. We want to call tonight and reserve the back bar at Bourbon Street."

"Yup, I'm free! Of course I'll be there. This is exciting," Cee knew where this was going and she wanted to make sure Lou couldn't tell that she was spooked.

"Great! We want everyone that's going to be in the bridal party to be there. We're going to give out little gifts just asking officially, even though I'm pretty sure everyone already knows."

"Sounds good. Do you know how you're going to ask?" Maybe if she just kept the conversation going in another direction Lou would back out and she could get to sleep tonight without knowing what was to come.

"I've been looking for something cute and simple on Pinterest, it's kind of last minute so I don't have a lot of time to make everything," Lou took a deep breath. "The invite wasn't the only reason I called, Cee."

"I know, Lou," Cee's voice was quiet, a bit of resignation that she couldn't fight creeping its way in.

"I'm sorry, Cee," she could tell that this conversation was hard for Lou and she felt for her friend. She'd seen the worst of it. Cee was sure that Lou didn't want to be the person to bring Max back into her life.

"It's okay. I knew it was going to happen eventually and it's going to be totally fine," Cee did her best to sound sure.

"It's just that Joe and him are really close now, like college close, and I couldn't ask him not to include him. It wouldn't be fair," Cee was sorry that Lou had even felt the need to do so.

"Lou, it's going to be fine. Even better than fine, we're

going to have a great night and then I'll know who's helping me plan the best bachelorette party to ever exist."

"Thank you, Cee. I know this might suck, but it means the world to me that you're going to be there."

"Louisiana, I wouldn't miss it for anything."

And she wouldn't have. She spent the week bouncing between nervous excitement and full on dread, but she knew that this was something she had to do. Her best friend was marrying Max's best friend, they would have to see one another again eventually. At least she had time to mentally prepare for it.

As was expected, Max consumed her thoughts in the days leading up to Thursday night. When she remembered him she could still see that handsome boy crossing the quad, eyes tired, asking her to lunch. And that was something to see. She closed her eyes again, that was really something to see. It's such a mistake to think that you can close a chapter and never return to it.

Her walk had come to a close and she was grateful for it. As she stared at the front door of the restaurant, she took just a moment to breathe in and out. She'd made it here and it had taken her longer than it should have, but she was ready now. He was on the other side of that door and she was about to walk right through it. And, no matter what happened next, it would affect her, it may even change her.

As she gripped the door handle and pulled it open, she thought about the years that she'd spent wondering when she would see him again and praying that it wasn't by chance or in a moment when she just plain wasn't ready. But she was prepared now and there he was standing not five feet away, laughing with a bottle of beer in his hand. And he turned towards Cecelia as the door swung shut behind her and the laughter died on his lips. And, just like that, Max Maylor was the lightning that struck her twice.

Cecelia found herself glued to the spot, her aching feet unable to take another step forward. Her bag felt heavy on her shoulder and her jacket was suddenly uncomfortably tight. Her eyes were locked on his, even as one of the guy's in his group slapped him on the shoulder, Max's gaze didn't waver.

Before she could move, Lou was grabbing Cee's arm and dragging her towards the bar, away from the spot where Max still stood.

"You're here! I was getting scared that you weren't going to make it," Lou quickly procured a vodka cranberry and shoved it into Cee's hand, eyeing her until she took a sip.

"Lou I told you I wasn't going to miss it!" Cee helped herself to another sip of her drink, feeling the tremble in her hand as the adrenaline left her body. He was here, just over her shoulder.

If she moved three steps to the right she'd be in his line of vision. She hated her awareness of his proximity, which fled back to her once she entered the room. It had nowhere near its old strength, but it was hanging in there. She wondered if she took those three steps, could she still feel his eyes on her the way she used to.

Cecelia shook her head. She needed to focus.

"How's it going? Is everyone here?"

Lou shot her an incredulous look.

"Cecelia? You're just going to ignore the fact that Max freaking Maylor is standing in this room right now? He looks like someone just dumped cold water on his head, you should see his face," Lou was taking quick glances over Cee's shoulder, assessing the situation.

"What do you want me to do, Lou? I knew he was going to be here, but this isn't about us. Is everyone here?" Cee drained her drink and quickly ordered another one.

"Downing those vodka crans a little quick for someone who has no stake in this night," Lou was smirking now. "And don't think I didn't notice how quickly that 'us' found it's way back into your vocabulary. You can pretend all you want, but I'm not leaving your side. Part of this night is about you, Cee, and I've got your back."

Cecelia could've cried from the relief she felt in that moment.

"Please don't, I don't know what I'll say if he comes over here," Cee grabbed Lou's hand. "You're the best friend in the world."

"Yes, I know," Lou gave Cee's hand a quick squeeze. "Just remember that when the wedding planning Google docs start rolling in. You look absolutely gorgeous by the way, like I didn't even recognize you for a second."

Cecelia let out her first laugh of the night.

"I really tried, Lou. And I'm completely and totally at your service, send those Google docs in bulk," she swore, and she meant it.

With that, Lou called over her two high school friends who'd be joining the wedding party and introduced Cecelia to them as her maid of honor, with a wink. Cecelia knew that Louisiana had been waiting for her to arrive before she officially began asking her friends if they'd do she and Joe the honor of being in their wedding party. Cecelia could just make out a box on a back table, filled with Pinterest-worthy gifts she was sure.

She was aware of Max and, thankfully, he seemed pinned to his spot so there wasn't any movement to account for. She wasn't sure how this was supposed to go. Should she suck it up and say hi to him? Did he even plan on approaching her? She knew she needed to break the ice at some point. As she'd said to Lou, this was just the beginning of what would likely be a year's worth of run-ins.

She decided not to think any further about it until she'd at least finished her second drink. She needed to chill out and slow down with the vodka or it would hit her all at once. So she traded her gulps for sips and mingled with the soon-to-be bridal party.

As was expected, the group of seven girls that Lou had assembled was filled with good people. Cee didn't foresee any cattiness arising, a fact that boded well for the bachelorette party planning and the wedding day as a whole.

It wasn't long before Louisiana and Joe found a spot in the center of the room, drawing the attention of the party with a spoon against Lou's champagne glass and quick shout from Joe.

"Hey, everyone," Lou's raised voice quieted the few murmurs that remained. "We just want to thank you all for being here tonight. It means the world to us to have you all here as we start planning one of the biggest days of our lives."

Everyone let out an excited word in Lou's direction confirming that they were just as happy to be here as she was to have them.

"So, without further ado, Joe and I would like to formally ask you all to be a part of our wedding day and stand beside us as we take this next step."

Lou reached for the box of gifts and walked towards her girls and Joe grabbed a single shopping bag from the box. Cee could make out the personalized cigar boxes as Joe began shaking hands with his crew, laughing at whatever it is that men say when they're trying to be appropriate and supportive.

Lou had put together small gift baskets with champagne glasses, mini bottles of Dom Pérignon, and beautiful white gold bracelets. It was simple and sweet and Cee could see the excited tears in Lou's eyes as everyone hugged her tight. As reluctant as she'd been to walk through that door, being here for her friend tonight was one thousand percent worth the effort.

It was in this moment that she turned her head to the right, hoping to catch Joe in a similar state of happiness, that she noticed Max walking slowly towards her. She caught his eye and gave a small nod, as if to confirm that, yes, now was as good a time as any. He smiled tentatively at her as he came to stand beside her.

She hadn't gotten a good look at him before, but she took a second to take him in now. How she'd forgotten how good the boy looked in dress pants, but remembered almost everything else, was beyond her. They were navy and tailored perfectly and he'd paired them with a light blue button down, sleeves rolled and cognac dress shoes.

His hair was shorter now, but not by much, and he looked so full and healthy. She could see it in his cheeks and shoulders and in the way that the buttons on his dress shirt sat firmly against his chest, rather than hanging off just that little bit.

"Hi, Cecelia," he looked like he might laugh at the ridiculous tension sitting between them. She wished he would, just to have something to cut through it.

"Hey, Max," Cecelia turned to face him fully, really meeting those eyes again for the first time. "Fancy meeting you here."

"Less fancy for me, I've been warned within an inch of my life to leave you alone," Cecelia noticed Joe watching them carefully, probably annoyed that Max had waited for the one moment that he would be distracted to approach Cecelia.

"Have you," Cee questioned quietly. "That seems a bit severe."

"It just felt ridiculous, to see you here and act like we'd never met," he looked quickly at the ground before meeting her eyes again. "If I'm bothering you, Cee, please just tell me and I'll walk away. I just figured we can't avoid one another forever, not with the wedding and everything."

"No, you're right," Cee agreed. "It would be weird to just ignore one another. And totally unnecessary. I'm glad to see you, Max. You look so well."

She didn't mean to so obviously bring up the past within seconds of speaking to him, but she had to say it. This was the man she'd been hoping to meet one day, the healthy man she thought might only be a dream. She wanted to acknowledge his progress, his victory in a hard-fought battle.

"Thanks, Cee," Max looked serious for a moment. "I'm doing well. I'm feeling really good these days, so thank you."

He was acknowledging something of his own with that.

"And you look great, too. You changed your hair," he was smiling again. "It looks nice like that. Very sophisticated."

"Thanks, I just cut it last weekend. It was kind of on a whim, but I'm really liking it," Cee ran a hand through the aforementioned locks. It was a nervous gesture and she hoped he hadn't caught it.

"And everything else is good?" Max took a sip of his beer.

"You're still working over at Grantham?"

"Yup, I'm still there. I ended up getting that column I was up for and it went well, so I haven't had a reason to look elsewhere," she felt awkward listing her successes when she had no idea if he was even working.

"That's great, Cee. I knew you'd get it. They would've been crazy not to pick you," there was something close to pride in his eyes and the familiarity of it twisted a knot in the center of her stomach.

"You're being nice, but I'm really happy with it. It was definitely a change, but I think I needed it. It's been good for me," Cecelia found herself looking anywhere but Max's eyes.

"What about you?" she quickly changed the subject before she could start rambling nervously about herself.

"I'm actually back in school believe it or not," he looked tired as he said it. Happy, but tired.

"Oh, yeah?" Cee was surprised. "Are you still going for law?"

"I am, yeah," Max hesitated before going on. "I actually ended up finishing out that semester, back when, well you know when. I really only had finals left at that point, so I just got through them and then didn't register for classes for the next semester. It took me a while to get back on track, but I'm just about done now. I'm going to be graduating in May if everything works out."

"Max," Cecelia could feel the emotion of this conversation finally hitting her. "Max, that's incredible. Really, really incredible."

"Thanks, Cee," he looked a bit overwhelmed himself. He finished his drink, placing the empty bottle on the bar beside him and checked her glass. "Can I get you another one?"

Cecelia nodded and sipped the last of her own drink as Max flagged down the bartender. She was grateful that he'd broken the moment; she didn't want to end up crying in front of him. Not here and not now.

Max dropped some cash on the bar as their drinks were

placed down in front of them and handed her a fresh cup before taking a swig of his own. He let out a nervous laugh.

"I feel weird," he turned quickly towards her. "Do you feel weird?"

"I honestly don't know how I feel," Cee let her shoulders relax. "I feel like I've never met you and like I've always known you, all at once."

"That's a good way of putting it," Max agreed. "Like I want to catch up with you, but this is just not our style, you know? Asking questions and giving these tentative answers. Can we just talk?"

"Yes, please," Cee finally let herself laugh. "I almost started crying for a second there. How embarrassing?"

"Honestly, me too," Max looked perplexed. "Imagine what those two would've done if they looked over and the two of us were just sobbing at the bar?"

Cecelia was cracking up; Lou would've flipped.

"I don't even want to think about Lou's reaction to that," Cee eyed her friend wearily across the room. "She's been stressed about us seeing one another again."

"Yeah, I got that from the many threats that Joe made on my life," Max shrugged. "They're just being good friends, but he got a little too detailed at one point. Something about ripping my eyeballs out."

"Ew, not your eyeballs! Those are the best part," Cee clamped her mouth shut as soon as the words were out. Why she couldn't have clamped it shut *before* she spoke was just her luck. And maybe the vodka had a bit to do with it, too.

Max looked very pleased with himself as he regarded her.

"The best part, huh?" he smirked.

"I shouldn't have said that. I think I'm drinking these too quickly," she tried to backtrack, but the mood had changed.

"Don't take it back now! I'm just enjoying the compliment," Max took a swig of his beer. "It's not everyday someone tells you what your best part is."

"Max," she groaned.

"I'm sorry, I'll stop," he held up his hands. "It's wiped from the record, you never said it."

"Thank you," Cee placed her drink on the bar and pushed it from her, a move that had Max laughing.

"So, moving on," Cee reached for the box that Max had set on the bar beside him. "What did Joe get you all? And who's the best man?"

"That would be a custom made cigar box filled with Cubans," Max popped the top, showing her the neatly placed wares inside. "And you're looking at him."

"No way," Cee's jaw dropped. "How'd you pull that one off?"

"Wow, I'll take that as a congratulations," he shot her a look, faking indignation. "And I happen to be Joe's oldest friend. I might've dropped off the map for a few years, but history has a way of erasing that, you know?"

He was regarding Cecelia now, trying to read her.

"Yeah, I do know a little bit about that," her voice had gone soft as she placed the cigar box back where it had been.

"It really is good to see you, Max," she grabbed onto the hand he had resting on the bar. "This is all I ever wanted, to see you like this."

"Cee, you have no idea," he gripped her hand. "I did everything I could to get here. I just can't believe you're even talking to me."

"I could say the same thing," she could feel her voice cracking. "The way I just left..."

"Cecelia, no," he shook his head. "That's not fair and we both know it. You only did what had to be done."

"Max," she was going to apologize again, she could feel it even though her instinct was to fight it.

"Cee, come on, let's go check in on the bride and groom," his own smile was teary. "We have a lot of responsibilities now. We can't forget them."

"Okay, you're right," Cee shook her head lightly, feeling the buzz that was clouding her thoughts. "I'll be sure to smile, so

Joe doesn't do anything to your eyes."

"That would be greatly appreciated," she could feel Max's hand on her lower back as he began leading them across the room. She noticed how his arm stiffened and dropped when he realized what he was doing, old habits already haunting them.

By the time they reached Lou and Joe, Lou's questioning gaze could only be described as penetrating. Cecelia wandered away from Max, towards the table where the tray of champagne had been placed. She picked up a flute just to have something to do with her hands.

Lou was beside her in seconds.

"Are you okay? Joe told him to leave you alone, to let you go to him when you were ready," Lou was clearly frustrated. "Of course, he can't listen to one simple request. Wouldn't be Max Maylor if he didn't just do whatever the hell he wanted."

"Lou, calm down. I'm totally fine and it needed to happen," Cee did her best to look unbothered even though her heart was still beating at an odd pace with no signs of regulating anytime soon. "We're going to be seeing a lot of each other. He is the best man after all."

"Ugh, sorry I didn't warn you about that one," Lou rolled her eyes. "I was hoping that Joe would change his mind last minute and ask his weirdo cousin from down the shore."

"Lou, I know that you still have a lot of ill feelings towards Max for everything that happened with us, but it doesn't seem like he's like that anymore," Cee implored. "He's the best man in your wedding, I don't want you having any issues with him on my account. Consider the air cleared between us."

"One conversation and the air is cleared?" Lou seemed incredulous.

"Yes, the air is cleared," Cee met Lou's eyes with a strong gaze. "Obviously there's history there and maybe things will be weird from time to time, but I'm going to be okay. We talked and I feel fine."

"You're sure you're okay? You're not just saying that?"

"Lou, you'd be able to tell if I was lying. I'm good," she shot her friend a smile. "This is the perfect party and I can't wait to start planning this wedding. Can we just focus on that?"

"If you insist," Lou laughed. "I already have so many ideas I haven't told you about. I'm going to write it all down when I get home tonight."

"Great, I can't wait to hear them," Cee squeezed Lou's arm. "It's going to be a beautiful wedding."

"I hope so," Lou glanced over her shoulder in time to catch Joe and his groomsmen taking a round of shots. "Seriously? He's going to be so sick tonight."

And with that, Lou rushed off to scold Joe. He just laughed and scooped her up in his arms, planting a sloppy kiss on her face as she dissolved into laughter.

Cee grabbed her water bottle from her bag and took a swig, capping and replacing it before shrugging her coat on. She'd had enough for one night, she thought. She quickly said her goodbyes, promising to call Lou in the morning. She found Max trying to force a glass of water into Joe's hand, and gave him a quick hug telling him again that it was good to see him before making her exit.

The air was cooler outside than when she'd entered the bar and she was grateful for the chill in her lungs as she took a deep breath and let it out slowly. She couldn't believe it was over. She couldn't believe she talked to Max, had a whole conversation with him, and felt peaceful about it. She stepped forward as the light on the corner up ahead turned green, throwing her hand in the air to catch an oncoming cab.

She smiled to herself as the cabbie switched off his vacancy light and pulled to a stop in front of her.

"Cecelia, wait!" she whipped her head around in time to see Max stepping out of the bar, the door swinging closed behind him.

"Max?"

"I know it's late, but do you want to grab a cup of coffee or food or something? There's a diner around the corner that's not too bad," he looked sure she would say no. It was as if he'd run out here in spite of himself, fully aware of the fact that he was pushing his luck past its limits.

She didn't answer right away and she could see the cabbie throwing up his hands out of the corner of her eye. *You coming, lady?*

"Please, Cee? I promise not to spill anything on you," he smiled hopefully at her, the same smile she'd seen for the first time in the bedroom of that frat house all those years ago. It was the FOMO on Cecelia smile and it was quite possibly more effective with the passage of time.

Cecelia nodded at Max and waved the cab off.

"Sure, I could go for some hot chocolate. It's finally starting to get colder out," she fell into step beside him.

"Yeah, finally," he was looking straight ahead, hands in his pockets. "I always think of you in the fall."

"Oh, just in the fall?" Cecelia wrapped her coat around herself, trapping the warmth inside.

"Yeah, strictly in the fall. It's like as soon as the leaves start turning I remember this girl. Takes a few days before I even realize it's you," Max hadn't worn a coat, but he didn't seem to be feeling the cold the same way that she was.

"I'm your fall girl. I'll take it," Max signaled them left at the corner and Cecelia was happy to follow along.

"Wouldn't want to be my summer girl, that's for sure," it was easier to talk like this, side by side, without having to look him in the face.

"That's for damn sure," she could see the diner up ahead and she glanced up at Max now to find him looking back down at her.

"Hate to tell you, but you're the year-round girl, Cee. Couldn't forget you in the summer, even if I tried," Max stopped short and reached for the door to the diner. There were just a few patrons scattered about, the sound of pots and pans drifting in from the kitchen overtook the quiet conversations.

Cecelia felt a certain calm envelope her as the waitress led them to a booth along the window and Max quickly excused himself to use the restroom. Seeing him had not been all that she had expected. The longing and sadness that she forethought did not dominate everything else that she felt at the sight of him, just a few feet away for the first time in too long. Much too long. In this moment of focus, her first in nearly a week, she felt thankful for the circumstances that ended their relationship.

Of all of the terrible decisions he'd made, he had never chosen to part from her. There had been no other woman receiving quickly deleted text messages or waiting for him to excuse himself from her presence for a few hours. She never had to meet his eyes and wonder where they had wandered. There was somehow more finality in an ending of that nature.

It was a direct message that something vital was missing from the relationship, whether it was his fault or hers. And the absence of that elusive "thing", which a person that strays can never quite put into words, leads to the circumstances which create the absence of trust, the elusive thing that everyone has the word, but never quite the stomach, for. With them, he had just as little trust in himself as she had in him, which was an allying factor rather than a dividing one.

She had no anger towards him and it would help them move forward. What they moved forward as was a question she couldn't even begin to answer. She felt the trouble more than sensed it. And she thought the reason for that might be because the trouble would be coming from her.

She hated feeling like she'd just been biding her time, like she was just waiting for him to come back around and she'd be taking care of the rest. She vowed to never drink around him again, at least not until the night of the wedding when it would be completely unavoidable.

She felt her stomach drop at the thought. Max in a suit, at the end of the aisle just as she'd always pictured him. The wedding night would be interesting, indeed. She looked up to see Max heading back toward the table and she sent him a small smile as he slid into the seat across from her.

"Hey," her voice was lower than she'd intended it to be.

"Hey," Max returned her smile before pulling the menu open on the table in front of him.

"You're not in the mood for food or anything?" he was skimming the appetizers, but she was sure he would get a burger. He always got a burger.

"I could maybe go for some pancakes. I skipped a few meals today and I think I'm finally starting to feel it," her stomach growled, as if on cue.

"By a few do you mean every meal? Because that's where I'm at right about now. I think I'm gonna go for a burger, maybe a milkshake, too," he hadn't looked up from the menu, but he would've seen a knowing smile spreading across Cee's face if he had.

"Okay, let's do it. A milkshake sounds good to me, too."

The waitress seemed to be waiting for Max to look up from the menu, if the way she rushed over as soon as it was closed was any sign. There was a beat after the food was ordered and the menus were gone that Max and Cecelia just looked at one another. There were lines on his face now that hadn't been there three years ago, small creases marking the passage of time. They looked good on him, somehow aging him in a way that made him even more handsome.

"Max," Cecelia began, but she wasn't sure what she wanted to say to him.

"Yeah?" He looked ready, like he'd been waiting for her to lay into him or freak out on him and now was the time.

"I don't know. Nothing," Cecelia fidgeted with the silverware in front of her.

"Whatever it is, I want you to say it. Don't hold anything back. We aren't strangers and I really don't want us acting like we are," the look on his face had morphed into something more serious than she'd seen in the bar.

"It doesn't feel that way, does it? Like we're strangers?" Cecelia met his eyes. "We haven't spoken a word to one another in nearly three years, but I feel like no time has passed at all. I really didn't expect it to feel like this and it's confusing the hell out of me."

"I know what you mean. I thought for sure things would be at least a little bit awkward, I think things *should* be awkward, but they just...aren't," he shrugged his shoulders.

"I know. I mean, I'm half grateful, but the other part of me is kind of scared. It feels like we were never apart and that's crazy because we're two different people," Cecelia let out a sigh of confusion. "I mean there's so much that's happened and changed that we should probably get into, but it just feels unnecessary. It's like we'll get there when we get there."

"I think it might be because we didn't draw it out," Max offered. "I noticed it the second we started talking at the bar, the way things just kind of fell back into place. But it makes sense if you think about it. We left on as good of a note as we could've for the situation we were in. There was a lot of respect in that, I think we really did ourselves a favor by cutting it there, just like that and maybe that's paying off for us now."

"Yeah, that does make sense. That was tough though, for me at least. I felt like I had so much more to say and I just never got to say it. I actually ended up going into a really dark place afterwards," she glanced up to find Max's face crumbling just a little bit.

"It was hard for me to get back on my feet. It wasn't you, or it wasn't *just* you, that triggered it," Cecelia tried her best to keep her voice steady as she continued.

"It was the realization that my life could very well turn out to be a lot less than I'd imagined. I starting seeing all of the ways things could go wrong, and the life that went along with all of those different turns made it hard to be happy. It just got really hard to be happy. It was really sad to remember things and have no one to share them with, and it was sad to forget things and have no one to remind you of them. It all just felt so wrong."

Max met her gaze and nodded his understanding.

"I'll never forget that feeling," he began. "Like you were the leader and all of the light and air were single file behind you, walking out of my life. I'll never forget it. I spent almost an entire year replaying it in my head before I actually acted on it and finally got clean."

"I had to do it, you know? I was doing everything in my power and it wasn't helping you, so I had to make a decision. I just couldn't really believe it was over afterwards. Sometimes I think it never fully hit me, not in my bones. I'm scared that's why things are like this between us still, because I could never really let it go."

"I've never left you, Cecelia. I never let you go. I know that I've disrespected you, and hurt you, and scared you, and it was my fault that we didn't work three years ago, but I never walked away. I couldn't do it back then, when it probably would've been for the best, and I don't think I'll ever be able to."

"I think I'm just trying to be smarter than I was. When we were together, it never crossed my mind that there would come a time when we *wouldn't* be together. And the way I left, it didn't feel final – it was desperate. And it took me a long time to accept that months were passing and it wasn't a temporary break. Even when you weren't my boyfriend anymore, I still thought of you as the man that would be my husband one day."

"Damn Cee, was this whole conversation just your completely convoluted way of proposing to me?" he got out the sentence before her palm connected with his chest, but barely.

"Max, be serious!"

"…Because I know we're two very modern people, total equals in every way and all that, but I feel a little weird about this."

He was full out laughing now, and Cee was trying not to join him, but she couldn't deny that it felt good to lighten the conversation that little bit. "I'm sorry, I'm sorry! I'll be serious, I promise."

"Seriously Cee, I never actually accepted that we weren't end game. I think you could be off married to some other guy, kids and all, and I'd still think of you as mine."

"I'm really happy I never had to see you with anyone else.

That would've really thrown me," Cecelia's voice was quiet. This conversation had turned into a roller coaster of sorts.

"There wasn't anything to see, I was kind of just working on me, working my way back to you," he shot her a quick look, and she could tell he was at least a little embarrassed about what was coming out of his mouth next. "I used to imagine what I would do if I saw you with someone else; all these different scenarios, from going nuts to being really stoic and respectful to win you back. I could never decide if I should play on your memories or show you what a nice, mature adult I turned out to be. What do you think would've gone over the best?"

"Eh, I don't think you would've had to overthink it. A good old 'Hey Juice' would've done the trick."

"Such a sucker for the classics. The memories, then."

"I do love the memories."

Max reached out his hand just then, weaving his fingers through hers, flexing them a bit in the familiar hold. Cecelia's mind went quiet. She wanted to feel this moment and to not overthink it. He was just touching her hand; it could be simple if she let it be.

The waitress came over with their food then, effectively separating their hands and killing the moment between them. Cecelia took a long sip of her milkshake, savoring the sweet taste of the chocolate as it cooled her mouth, before digging into her pancakes. Max's burger was half gone before she'd even gotten a bite of them.

"Sorry," he said as he swallowed a bite. "I wasn't kidding, I really haven't eaten all day."

"Me neither. I think I was too nervous thinking about tonight."

"I *know* I was too nervous thinking about tonight," Max popped a fry into his mouth. "I had my mom help me pick out this outfit, I think it made her week."

"Well, tell her she did a good job," Cecelia shot Max a wink, watching as his smile hit his eyes.

"Hey now, she only helped me pick which combo to wear.

I put all of this together myself," he gestured to his shirt, as if he'd stitched it with his own two hands.

"Okay, well then tell yourself you did a good job," Cecelia took another bite of her pancakes, already growing full. "How is your mom doing anyway? And your dad and Isabella?"

"They're good, no thanks to me," he let out a humorless laugh. "My parents are pretty much the same, I think my mom is going to retire after this year which is good. And Bella is at FIT now. I'm actually crashing at her apartment tonight so I can just shoot into Newark in the morning on the train."

"Oh wow, Bella at college," Cecelia let out a whistle. "We. Are. Old."

"Getting there, yeah."

"That's good for your mom, she deserves a little time off to relax."

"Yeah, no one deserves it more," Max's expression changed. "She told me she saw you. I mean, she didn't tell me when it happened, but when I told her about tonight she mentioned it to me. Told me not to tell you of course, but that seems less important now than I guess it was back then."

"Yeah, she called me a few months after we broke up," Cecelia didn't feel as awkward talking about it as she might've if this night hadn't already been so weird. "She just wanted to know if I could tell her anything about you. It was kind of nice to see her though. It was as close to seeing you as I'd gotten in a long time and it made me feel better. I couldn't stand the fact that our last conversation had gone like that. I thought for sure we'd drag it on for longer or even accidentally run into one another in those first few weeks."

"I know what you mean. To go from talking and seeing each other every single day for years and then just to cut it cold turkey? I think I turned my phone off for like a month because it was too weird not to call you," Max had finished his burger and was just picking at his fries, probably looking for the burnt ones.

"I actually deleted your phone number," Cecelia admitted. "I didn't think I could keep myself from calling you."

"What a number we did on each other, huh?" Max shook his head. "It was for the best though, right? You're good? You're happy?"

"I am. I really like my life and I'm proud of my career," Cecelia hesitated for a moment. "But I would be lying if I didn't say that I'm happier, sitting here with you, than I have been in a long time."

"I feel the same way," he glanced down at the table. "And I want you to know that I've been clean for almost two years. I know that you really have no reason to trust me, and I don't even know how much it matters to you, but I need you to know that I did it."

"It matters to me," there were tears in Cecelia's eyes. "It's always mattered to me."

"I put my family through hell for about a year and then I just stopped. I made the decision that I was done and I haven't taken anything since," Max's phone was buzzing on the table but he ignored it. Cee could see Joe's name flashing across the screen. "I was in an out-patient program and I went to meetings with a counselor and I finally made it here."

"Thank God, Max," Cecelia reached across the table and put a hand on Max's arm. "I was so scared that I would get here tonight and I would see that you weren't okay. I think it would've ruined me."

"I wanted to call you," Max shifted in the booth, leaning just that little bit closer. "I've thought about it a lot over the past year, but I kept chickening out."

"I get it, I don't think I would've been able to reach out either, if I were you," Cecelia nodded. "There's just so much history and so many ways that this could've gone."

"Exactly," Max sighed. "This is more than I could've asked for. No matter what happens, just for it to be okay between us, it's like a weight off my shoulders."

"We pulled it together, Max," Cecelia squeezed his arm before leaning back and letting a yawn out.

"Tired?" Max reached for his phone, lighting up the screen

to check the time. "Damn, it's almost 1. We've been here for a while."

"One? Oh god," Cecelia groaned. "Work is going to be fun tomorrow."

"I guess we should go?" He seemed hesitant, as if the suggestion alone was hard to swallow.

"Yeah, I think I'm just going to call an Uber," Cecelia reached for her wallet, but Max waved her off.

"I got it, Cee. Why don't you call your car, I'll head up to the register and take care of the bill."

"Okay, thanks Max," she pulled out her phone, opening the Uber app and requesting a car.

"Did you get one?" Max questioned as he walked back to the booth.

"I did," Cecelia glanced at her phone. "Three minutes."

"Quick," Max said quietly.

"Yup," Cecelia slid out of the booth and stood in front of Max, meeting his eyes.

"Really quick," he cleared his throat.

"I know," she breathed out.

Max didn't say anything for a moment, just stared at her.

"I'll walk you out, Cecelia," he gestured for her to lead the way, reaching ahead of her to swing open the door as they left.

Her Uber was pulling up as they stepped outside. Max stopped in front of the car, pulling open the door to the back seat before turning towards her.

"Thanks for coming with me, Cee," he was tired too, she could see it in his eyes.

"Max," Cecelia trailed off, not sure what to say.

"I'll talk to you, okay?" She knew what he was asking.

"Yes. Yes, definitely," The hope was clear in her voice and Max seemed to notice.

Max leaned down and left a quick kiss on her cheek.

"Goodnight, Cecelia."

"Night, Max."

And with that, she climbed into the back of the Uber and

Max gently shut the door. Cee watched through the car window as he stepped back onto the curb, giving a little wave. She returned it as the car picked up speed and the city became a blur around her. She clutched her purse tightly in her hands and took a deep breath.

That was that.

2018
September

Her alarm went off at 7 am sharp the next morning, despite the fact that she felt like her head had just hit the pillow. She picked it up, planning to snooze it for just a few minutes. Her body needed just a little while longer and then she'd be able to get through the day.

She blinked twice at the screen before she realized the text was really there. It was a number she'd deleted, but would always remember. Cecelia sat up in bed, her exhaustion seemingly disappearing into thin air. Her heart sped up as she unlocked her phone and opened her messages, a smile spreading wide across her face as she read the words in front of her.

Morning Cee - just wanted to give you my number. You'll be needing it.

Made in United States
North Haven, CT
12 April 2022